Cherry Cobbler

JoHannah Reardon

Copyright © 2012 JoHannah Reardon

All rights reserved.

ISBN-13: 978-1475117691
ISBN-10: 1475117698

DEDICATION

To my niece, Ann, who encouraged me that this book was worthwhile and gave me my first positive review.

1

"Where's Papa going with that ax?" That's how the book *Charlotte's Web* begins. You know—the story where the spider saves Wilbur the pig from becoming bacon. I used to cry whenever I read that book as a child. Every time the pig cried, I cried too. Maybe it was because I was rather plump myself and identified too strongly with the main character.

At any rate, that's kind of how I feel now. Just like Wilbur, blubbering because he's about to become someone's breakfast. Not that I'm physically in danger. Not at all. I'm plugging away quite well as far as that goes. No threats on my life, no fatal diseases. In fact, I escaped without even a cold when everyone else called in sick at work. No, my problems are more of the social nature.

Now don't get me wrong. I'm a likeable individual with lots of friends, always the first person to get invited to a party. I often end up in the middle of the room with a crowd gathered around as I tell jokes and generally keep everyone from giving up and going home. Some of my friends plan their parties around me the way they'd plan around a magician or singer they'd invited. So my problem is not being popular. I really am. The trouble is that I'm getting to an age where I want to settle down.

I'm twenty-eight years old. If you are any older than that, I'm sure you think I'm quite young. If you are under nineteen, it probably sounds close to death. I don't feel young or close to death, just tired of the carefree single life. There's nothing I'd like more than staying home with my man for a video and some popcorn.

Okay, now it's out. It's the man part I'm missing. I know. These days, women are supposed to be independent. They're not supposed to need men. At least that's the message I got as I slugged my way through college. But you know what? Even if we don't need them, they're kind of nice to have around. There are moments at work where I'd trade seven emotional females for one levelheaded male.

I work as a secretary at a garden center. Excuse me, as an administrative assistant. I think everyone gives workers fancy titles these days so they won't have to give them a raise. At least that's what my mom says. When I told her I'd been hired as an administrative assistant, I said it all hoity-toity like it was something important, but she said, "Hrmph. Your dad and I worked all those years to put you through college so you could be a secretary?" Fancy titles never fool Mom.

I went to college to be a teacher. It sounded nice; put together exceptionally motivating lesson plans, give the kids lots of hugs, be a hero. Yea right! I just about got killed during student teaching. Those kids saw right

Cherry Cobbler

through me. I don't know what I was thinking. I never even liked babysitting.

So after graduating, I stuck my teaching certificate in a drawer and haven't seen it since. I got a job at the garden center I'd pulled weeds at during college to make some extra cash. They liked me there and I could still hang around my college buddies. But now most of them are gone and I'm still here, looking for more meaning than filing forms and making phone calls.

The good part about staying around is that I stayed involved in my church. I'm from a small town originally so when I first went to Faith Church, I thought I'd died and gone to heaven. There were people galore, great music, a bazillion programs, and lots of eligible college men running around. I felt certain that I'd find The One at any turn. Ten years later, that idea is growing a little thin.

Don't misunderstand me. I still love Faith Church. I go to a Bible study every week, show up at every women's event the church sponsors and faithfully attend anything that has to do with food, always my weakness. I even volunteer in the nursery once in a while, which gives credence to the verse that says, "I can do everything through him who gives me strength." But the amount of available men has dwindled considerably. Those college men look like my kid brother to me and the older men, like my dad. The only men in my age range who aren't tied down have been married several times already or are spending most of their evenings at Alcoholics Anonymous. I'm glad they're at church, but I try not to spend too much time talking to them.

Not that they notice me either. I'm not bad looking. I have dark brown hair that used to be shoulder length but is now cut short into what my mom used to call a pixie cut. I still battle my weight although I'm not huge. Size sixteen is only slightly above average from everything I've read. I'm not too tall; in fact I'm kind of on the short side, which I've traditionally blamed my weight on. You know, I don't weigh too much; I'm just not tall enough. I try to keep up on the latest fashions although I've got to admit I've gotten behind a bit on that lately. So why don't they notice me? I've asked myself that question for years.

Do you know I haven't had even one real boyfriend? Well, unless you count Jordan in seventh and eighth grade. Those years were glorious for me. When everyone else was getting braces and glasses, I suddenly slimmed down for about eighteen months and blossomed. The trouble was, I didn't quit blossoming in ninth grade and I outsized Jordan by a good bit. That's when I became a size sixteen. I guess I could be proud of the fact that I'm the same size as when I was fourteen. Not too many women can say that. The odds have to work in my favor sometime.

There are occasions when I get frustrated about my standards. I decided years ago, that I would only marry a man who loved God with all his heart. It really wasn't too hard of a decision to make. After all, it wasn't like I was turning down men left and right. Our youth pastor talked about how important it was that we marry someone like-minded on the subject of God, and the one thing I knew was that I loved God. So I began to eliminate potential mates right there and then. And do you know what? I eliminated them all! I couldn't find one guy who loved God as much as I did, until I went to college. Then there were plenty at Faith Church, but no one asked me out. I fell in love at least three times and none of those guys even knew I existed, which probably calls into question the nature of my love. Anyway, I adjusted to this state of affairs pretty well for the last ten years until Todd started coming to the Bible study I attend.

Todd fits my profile of the perfect man. He's thirty-two, 5-foot-10, has sandy brown hair and a large, rugged build and spent the last 10 years as a missionary in Nigeria. How cool is that! He returned from the mission field because he was lonely and tired and needed a break. Well, I know someone who can help with at least the first part of that problem!

So why, do you ask, am I so blue? Because Todd has never been more than polite to me, and I've already decided that I want to marry him and help him reach Africa for Christ! Oh man, it's going to be a tough Bible study from now on.

Oh, one other thing. My name is Cherry. Now why would a parent do a thing like that?

2

"Cherry, are you going to the concert tonight at church? Our whole Bible study will sit together if you can come." I pictured Jeannie looking at me from her perfect blue eyes, blond hair and size eight dress. I tried not to resent her for that at the moment. I really did like her.

"Everyone's coming?" Darn. Was I too obvious?

"I think so."

"Yea, I can come." I still couldn't believe that we got such amazing artists at Faith Church, and I argued with myself that I wanted to go for the music and not in hopes that I'd sit next to Todd. Everything about him made me feel like I was back in junior high.

"Good. Then afterwards we can come over to our house. Would you mind making that wonderful bean dip you always whip up?"

"Sure, I'd be glad too. Anything else?"

"No, that should do it."

"Okay, see you there tonight."

I hung up the phone just in time to see Mrs. Vanderweide glowering at me. Her hair was dyed bright red now, a change from the frosted look she had last month. Both colors fit her personality. She had on a new fur jacket even though it was March and a bit warm for fur. Her skirt was leather and much too short for her chubby knees. "Cherry, I want to see Mr. Hopkins right now." Mrs. Vanderweide was one of the few people who loved my name and said it with a lilt like she was singing it.

"He's out on a job right now, Mrs. Vanderweide. Would you like to make an appointment?" I said it with a smile but braced myself for the blast that was coming, the way someone would hold a door against a strong wind.

She surprised me. "That's okay. I'll wait. I brought my phone, computer, and make-up kit. I'll just sit right over there until he gets in."

I couldn't imagine that she could get any more makeup on her face. She had her own line of cosmetics and tried to advertise all the shades at once. As she settled into the corner, unloading her bag around her, I felt a chill go through me. Poor Mr. Hopkins. This couldn't be good. He'd been so thrilled when she'd hired him to landscape her estate a few years ago, but no amount of money could make up for the grief she'd caused him since. He would design something and she'd tear it up while he started over. Finally, he found a layout she liked but when it was planted, she changed her mind and tore it all out. This was the third time she'd been in the last month.

Cherry Cobbler

"Why don't you let me try my new lipstick shade on you, Cherry? You always wear that pale shade. You'd look so cute in this bright color. Subtle is out, you know. Vibrant is in."

Vibrant has always been in for you, I thought. *Not a subtle bone in your body.* "Thanks, Mrs. Vanderweide, but I've got too much to do."

"Nonsense! You've got a minute to put this lipstick on."

Oh brother. Here we go. I knew there was no way out of it. She jumped up, acting very spry for her forty plus years, and yanked my chin up as she applied the way-too-bright color to my lips. "There, that's perfect. I'll just give you this sample so you'll know what shade to buy when you go to the store. Now, one of my competitors has a similar shade, but it's not the quality of my cosmetics. Don't be afraid of the high price. It's worth it. Don't forget now."

I nodded and put my head back down. When her cell phone rang, I quickly rubbed at my lips with a tissue. Glancing out the window, I noticed Mr. Hopkins getting out of the car. I quickly dialed his cell phone and whispered, "Just wanted to warn you. Mrs. V is waiting."

"Oh joy. Thanks for warning me. Nothing like a good day gone bad." I could see his face through the window. He looked as if he'd sucked on a lemon. I said a quick prayer for him and hung up the phone.

I watched him as he snuck in through the back way. Evidently Mrs. Vanderweide was too busy yelling at whoever was on the phone to notice. After a few minutes, Mr. Hopkins rang me. "I might as well get it over with. Send her in."

Mrs. Vanderweide had just finished her conversation and was plucking her eyebrows. I cleared my voice and plunged ahead. "Mr. Hopkins is in now. He said for you to come on back."

She gave me a smile that looked like Cruella De Vil when she's thinking about making a coat out of those Dalmatian puppies. She gathered everything together, stood up with a wiggle, and sauntered over to my desk. "You're the one who sends out the billing, right?"

"Yes."

"Well, I've been thinking." She paused and looked up toward the ceiling as if to demonstrate what thinking looked like. "Since I spend so much money here, I'd appreciate it if you would send a self-addressed, stamped envelope with the bill. I'll expect it next month." She gave me another sickly sweet smile and walked past me like the queen of Sheba.

"Oh brother," I said out loud as soon as she was out of earshot. It felt good to say something of what I felt out loud even if only God and I heard it. "Any way to gain a little more power and she does it. Save her, Lord. Save her from herself." I shook my head and turned back to the computer. I was working on a new flyer we were getting ready to send out. This was my favorite part of my job - the creative part. The worst part was wearing shades of lipstick I didn't like.

The day ended without much more ado. Mr. Hopkins reported that he was now redesigning Mrs. Vanderweide's pool area. He sighed when he told me, fully expecting that he would have to do it over several times. I gave him sympathetic murmurings and closed up shop.

One nice thing about my job is that when I leave for the day, I never give it another thought. Mrs. Vanderweide became a distant memory like a B movie that's forgotten as soon as you leave the theater. I hurried home to make my famous bean dip, stopping at the store for tortilla chips. I arrived at the church with thousands of others who were chatting and expectant. As soon as I was through the doors, I saw Jeannie waving to me. She smiled next to her lawyer husband, looking like the perfect wife that she was. How we became friends still amazes me. We met at a women's ministry fair and found out we both loved drama. We've been working together ever since on the drama team at church and studying the Bible together in her home. She accepted me with all my flaws and I accepted her with all her perfections. It's a beautiful relationship.

"How was your day, Cherry?"

"Only a little crazy, which is saying a lot."

"I think I'll come in and see you tomorrow. The gift shop there is the only place I can buy that fertilizer I like for my house plants."

"Tomorrow's Saturday. I won't be there."

"Oh, that's right. I'll come in sometime next week then."

We continued on with small talk until Todd walked in. All of a sudden my throat closed up and I started tapping my foot nervously. When I began wringing my hands together, Jeannie grabbed them. "What's wrong, Cherry? You look like you just saw a ghost."

"Oh great," I thought, "Todd's going to really love me if I go into a cold sweat each time he enters the room." I laughed and consciously relaxed every part of my body, refusing to look at him. "I'm fine, Jeannie. I guess I just need to sit down and enjoy the concert."

Mark and Sarah came in, followed by John and Megan. Both couples are about my age. I haven't gotten to know Sarah as well as Megan, but I like them both. Sarah had a baby, which pretty well took her out of my circle. "Good, we're all here," I thought.

As we turned to go in, Grant ran up to us with Josh in tow. "Oh wow. I was afraid we were too late to catch you before you went in. I'm glad we didn't miss you." He

Cherry Cobbler

smiled a big grin, like an undersized golden retriever. Josh followed him like a puppy; the two were inseparable. We all smiled back and Jeannie's husband, Jeff, threw an arm around Josh, treating him like a long lost friend. Grant and Josh are always late.

I've known both these guys for years, but they're in that category of men I try to avoid. I just don't want to encourage them or have them get any wrong ideas. Grant's a nice guy, but definitely not my type. He's only a few inches taller than me and remember I'm short. His dark brown hair is rarely combed neatly and usually falls over his eyes in a way that annoys me to no end. He wears glasses that went out of style about five years ago and his wardrobe is no better. Worst of all, he's in that former alcoholic group that I avoid like the plague. He's been clean as long as I've known him, but the whole thing scares me. I guess his personality is okay, but I've never gotten to know him so I can't really say.

Josh is a little better. He's very quiet and unobtrusive, follows style trends a little closer than Grant, and is about five inches taller. I don't know him that well either. I've always stuck to the women in our group until Todd showed up.

When we walked into the auditorium, it was so crowded that we couldn't all sit together. We divided into two groups and I made sure I was in Todd's group. By some miracle, it worked out that I sat right next to him. It was perfect. Jeannie on one side, Todd on the other. We chatted for a few minutes until the concert began.

After that, we all lost track of time. The concert was amazing. even better in person than on the countless CDs of his that I owned. But in spite of all that, I couldn't help glancing over at Todd. He was amazing looking. Finally it dawned on me. He looks like a young Indiana Jones. That's it. After that, I kept glancing at him to see how he was reacting to everything. I laughed when he laughed. I grew serious when he did. I became very conscious of how I looked and straightened my hair and skirt several times until I caught myself and forced my attention back to the concert.

When it was over, we all headed for Jeff and Jeannie's house. After removing coats and setting out food, we sat around the living room chatting about the concert. Todd, as usual, had the most profound things to say. "I still can't get over the wealth of resources we have here. All those years in Nigeria, if I'd heard one concert like this, it would have carried me for days. I'll never take anything for granted again."

"You're right, Todd," Jeff added. "We're lucky to have you to remind us. Maybe you can take us on a vision trip there sometime."

"I'll go!" I yelled like I was at the ballpark. I said it so loud that I made everyone jump. Embarrassed by my outburst, I lowered my voice and added, "I've always been interested in missionary work," which made me wince inside because I knew perfectly well that I'd never been interested until Todd came along, but now it sounded like my dream job. I wondered if I'd get struck dead for lying like Ananias and Sapphira.

Todd barely noticed me. "That's a great idea. Maybe we can work that out this summer. We'd have to raise a lot of money, though."

"I've got some money set aside." Grant's voice was so low that most of us didn't notice him. "Me too," said Josh, always echoing Grant. Jeff nodded his head but turned back to Todd. "We'll find a way if that's what God wants us to do. Let's all pray about it."

I felt my heart sink a little. As soon as something was relegated to praying about it, it rarely got done, it seemed to me. But then again, who can argue with praying? I just knew that wherever Todd wanted to go, I wanted to be there too.

When the evening ended, I looked for a way to strike up a conversation with Todd. Just as I thought of an opening line, I felt someone take my elbow. "Can I walk you out to your car, Cherry?"

I looked at Grant in annoyance. Why was he bothering me? He made me forget my train of thought. "I'm not quite ready to go yet, Grant. I wanted to talk to Todd about a possible date for a vision trip to Africa."

Grant smiled, making him look like a little boy about to enter the candy shop. "That's a great idea, isn't it? Our Bible study would change for good if we did something like that together." I nodded distractedly as he added, "You're very brave to want to go. I know a lot of women who would be terrified to do something like that."

"Yea, that's me, a female Stanley Livingston. Or do I mean Arnold Swartzenegger? I get those two guys mixed up."

Grant looked at me in confusion so I took the opportunity to walk away and nab Todd.

3

The trouble with being in love is that it pretty well dominates everything. The next day, Saturday, which usually consists of cleaning my apartment, grocery shopping, and reading a good book, was now replaced by daydreaming about being a missionary in Africa. I spent the morning on the Internet, finding out everything possible about Nigeria. I checked into the missionary organization that Todd had gone with and made some calls to our local soup kitchen because I knew African Americans ran it and figured if I volunteered there, I'd be better prepared for the mission field.

Now all of this sounds good on the surface, but sometime during the day, I realized that I'd gotten the cart before the horse. In fact, it was running downhill and dragging that horse by the neck, about to strangle it. So I slowed down and made myself sit still. God, you are going to have to take over here. If you want me to be a missionary, I need to go whether Todd does or not. But I just don't know if I have what it takes to go it alone, God. It would be so nice to go with someone. Preferably someone about five-foot-ten, with sandy hair. I smiled to myself. My absolute belief that God had a sense of humor held me in good stead now.

Anyway, I was able to salvage the day, get a few things done, and enjoy the evening chatting on the phone with some old college friends. The next day I got ready for church, trying not to pay too much attention to my appearance and concentrating on getting something out of the sermon rather than seeing Todd. It worked really well because Todd wasn't there, at least not at the service I was at, so I had a wonderful morning and learned that God was always on the throne no matter what my circumstances (the subject of the sermon). This helped focus me considerably and I spent my Sunday doing other things than thinking about Todd, at least most of the time.

Unfortunately, Grant and Josh were at church and decided to sit on either side of me. I don't know why they made me so nervous. They were certainly less obnoxious than my kid brother. I think it was the alcohol thing. After church when they talked about an AA meeting they were going to that night, I asked Grant, "Why do you two still have to go to those meetings? You've been clean a long time."

Grant looked me in the eye until I became uncomfortable. He was always doing that, like he could look right into my soul. It made me squirm. "More than anything, we like to be there to help encourage others. We know more than anyone how much help they need."

I nodded my head, glad there were guys like Grant and Josh looking out for others, but I still didn't want anything to do with it. My only experience with an alcoholic was an uncle who used to go on binges then show up and sleep it off at our house because his wife wouldn't let him back in. It was enough for me to vow I'd never date an alcoholic. I wanted a husband I didn't have to lock the door on and steal his key.

Monday dawned with a deluge. I ran to my car feeling like a cartoon character that was being chased by lightning. I've never seen the sky light up so much and the thunder was so loud that the ground shook. I love March.

I arrived inside the office all soggy. Fortunately my short haircut just needed a little shaping and it was good as new. My shoes were a little soggy though, so I slipped them off when I sat down to my desk. I was just getting comfortable when the phone rang. "Hello, Cherry?"

"Yes?"

"This is Roslyn."

"Roslyn! You're back. How long have you been home?"

"For about a week. I've been sleeping most of the time, but I woke up today feeling refreshed. Can we get together for lunch?"

"You bet. I'm dying to hear all about Romania. Your emails helped but being able to talk to you in person will be ten times better."

"Yes, it will. I long to hear your laugh again. There were times I wished I could ship you over with me so that I wouldn't take myself so seriously."

"Aw, that's nice." I never knew how to take compliments. "Where do you want to eat?"

"How about Eddie's, for old times sake?"

"Great! My treat."

"Thanks, Cherry. See you there at noon."

I set the phone down and sighed. Roslyn was my roommate in college and as opposite from me as Einstein is from Bozo. She studied to be a doctor and loved science classes and took math just for fun. I, on the other hand, majored in elementary ed, mostly because I could read children's books. What the gods of roommate placement could possibly have been thinking, I can't imagine. But the one and only true God knew exactly what He was doing. Roslyn started coming to church with me and became a Christian. After medical school, she did part of her internship in Romania where she'd been for the past year. I couldn't wait to see her again. We were like peanut butter and jelly, so different and yet smooth and creamy together.

Cherry Cobbler

The morning passed uneventfully. The rain subsided and the normal trickle of customers came in to see our designers. My favorite was Mrs. Johnson. "Hello. I'm looking for someone to help me landscape my new house."

"You've come to the right place. What exactly are you looking for?"

"Actually, I want all plants that I don't have to water. Do you have anything like that?"

I must have stared at her for an exceptionally long time because she finally spoke again.

"Like mums. Do you have to water those?"

"All plants need water, ma'am. There are no plants that live without water."

"Oh, my. How inconvenient. You'd think someone would have invented such a thing by now."

I nodded and smiled because that's my job, but it made the mission field seem all the more appealing. Surely no one in Africa thought that plants could live without water. All of sudden, spoiled Americans seemed like a despicable lot all together. I was proud of myself that I'd thought about that without thinking about Todd. Almost.

So I slipped on my soggy shoes, which had dried out at least a little, and headed for Eddie's, our favorite hang-out from college days. No one made a deli sandwich like Eddie and he knew every customer who walked through the door. Today he waved to me, and when Roslyn followed me in and we embraced, Eddie came out from behind the counter and put his big burly arms around both of us. It was just like old times.

We gave him our order and he insisted on treating Roslyn since she'd been gone so long. We settled into a table in the corner and picked up as if we'd only been here yesterday. "I'm sure everyone is asking you to tell everything that happened in an entire year, so I'll just sit here and let you guide the conversation to whatever you feel like talking about."

"That's what I love about you. You know me." She stretched in her chair and ran a hand through her tight curls. Roslyn was one of those women who could be beautiful if she ever took a minute to notice, but physical appearance meant nothing to her. "It was an incredible year. I'll never be the same. Working with the Romanian orphans has changed me forever. I don't know if I can go back to being a regular doctor now, sitting in a sterilized office, making all my patients come to me. The need there is desperate."

I nodded, not sure what to add, so Roslyn continued, "But, I'm going to have to decide. My parents don't mind me back for a while, but I'm sure they don't want me as a permanent fixture." She smiled and dimples popped up on her face. A casual observer would have no idea what she'd been through in the last year. She reminded me of Shirley Temple at this moment. But then, Shirley Temple grew up to be an ambassador so maybe I wasn't too far off.

"What would keep you from going back?"

"Ah, the million dollar question." Our food came so we both grew quiet while the waitress set our plates down. Even after the waitress left, Roslyn sat there tapping her forehead. "I think fellowship. I missed the fellowship here more than I can say. If I could have a team of people around me, I'd be okay. I guess it's something I'm going to have to duke out with God."

That was a phrase that was almost a code word between us. We first talked about having to duke things out with God when we read about Jacob and how he wrestled with God until morning. We decided that when we were having a tough time giving in to what God wanted, we'd just have to duke it out with him. I hadn't heard that phrase since Roslyn had left and it warmed my heart to hear it now.

"So, you feel like God may want you to go back, but you're not sure that's what you want?"

"Kind of. One part of me wants to go more than anything. I guess I feel like I just need to wait a bit to catch my breath." After pausing a moment more she broke into another smile, "Let's talk about something else. How're things at work?"

"Crazy, as usual." I glanced at her and decided to go for it. "Actually, I've been thinking some about the mission field."

"You?" Her eyebrows shot up and her eyes looked like some night animal.

"Is that so unbelievable?" I must admit her response hurt a bit. I didn't think she saw me as shallow.

"No." Roslyn seemed to struggle a minute. She scrunched her eyebrows together and looked as if she'd just swallowed something that got stuck in her throat. "I've just never heard you mention that before."

"It's a new thought, I've got to admit. Of course, I'm just in the early stages of thinking about it." There was no way I was going to tell her that Todd was my motivation. She'd shake her head in bewilderment at me if I did. I've seen that look on her face before. We passed the rest of lunch talking about less momentous things and when we finished, agreed to get together over the weekend. Seeing her again was like having the first daffodils of spring come out.

4

I should have known that I wouldn't be able to keep anything from Roslyn. We went out for dinner and to a movie on Saturday night. Afterwards as we sipped cappuccinos, which pretty well ruled out either of us getting any sleep that night, she said, "So, out with it. What in the world makes you think you want to be a missionary?"

For some reason I thought I could fudge around the question. "Well, you know. You had such a great experience in Romania and..." I took a big sip of my cappuccino to stall for time, but it wasn't enough. I should have bought that piece of shortbread. "And, you know, working at the Garden Center is not the most exciting life in the world. And, I want to help people. That's the best reason, isn't it?" I smiled real big as if to dazzle her so that she wouldn't be able to think of anything else to ask me.

It didn't work. In spite of my blazing pearly whites, she gave me that look that showed she wasn't buying any of it. Her head was tilting down, her eyebrows scrunched together and her mouth in a sort of pout. "You've never been to another country. It's not like here, you know. Conditions are a lot rougher. You don't even like to camp."

My smile faded away like so much sugar left in the rain. My tone became indignant. "I read *National Geographic* and I certainly won't be camping. Even in Africa they have houses."

Now her face jutted forward, her eyes wide and her mouth even wider. "You're thinking of going to Africa?"

I almost winced because of the incredulity that dripped from her voice. "Is that so amazing?"

"Yes, it is. When you said 'missionary', I pictured a South Seas island or something. That seems more your style."

"Well, maybe I've changed."

"Yea, and maybe aliens took over your body and I'm talking to someone from Jupiter."

Anyone else saying that would have made me mad, but Roslyn had earned the right to be brutally honest with me and after all, she was right. "Okay. You win. I met a guy."

Her eyebrows went up and a sly smile crept across her face. "Ah, everything is becoming clear now. So this guy is a missionary in Africa?"

I just nodded, returning the rather guilty smile.

Cherry Cobbler

"So, is it serious?"

My smile felt like it was actually dripping down into a frown. "No. He's never even asked me out."

Roslyn's expression changed to pity, which made me feel worse than when she was sneering at me. "Ah, Cherry, why do you do these things to yourself?"

I protested too loudly, sounding like a five-year-old even to myself. "It's not like that this time. I really think we'd be a great team. I just have to convince him."

"When will you learn that men can't be convinced? It's either there, or it isn't."

"I don't think that's true. If he could see that I'm passionate about his work, he might really notice me."

Roslyn just shook her head. "This must be some guy to get you thinking about being a missionary."

"Oh, he is. He's dreamy...my ideal man. Not only gorgeous but helps others. He works with AIDS patients. That has to be so meaningful." I looked out at the traffic flowing by, feeling that it summed up my life. "I have to admit, I'd never be a missionary on my own. But I think I could do it if I was crazy enough about the guy." I said it almost as a question, willing her to agree with me. Not a chance.

"I don't think so, Cherry, but knowing you, you aren't going to listen to me anyway so best of luck." She raised her mug as if to toast me.

I smiled and raised mine too. This time she was wrong. This time I'd show her. "What about you? Don't you ever want to get married?"

"Of course, but I have the opposite problem. How many men want to marry a doctor who's considering living in Romania? It rather narrows the field."

"See? That's probably just what Todd is thinking."

Roslyn didn't even dignify that statement with a denial. She just smirked.

Bible Study met on Wednesday night. My conversation with Roslyn changed my strategy. Maybe Todd needed to see I was interested. He was probably wishing he could find someone but never imagined that I might be willing to go to Africa. I'd show him that I was the one for him.

It took some maneuvering. I had to wait until the study was over and time it so that I was walking out just when he was. I happened to be in the middle of a story I was relating to Jeannie, so I had to end it rather abruptly and make some excuse to leave right away. Jeannie looked a little puzzled but turned to Sarah and let me slip out.

Cherry Cobbler

I caught up with Todd just ten yards from his car. I had to run to make it in time. His strides were long and athletic. Just seeing him walk made my heart do flip flops. He was one beautiful man. "Todd," I called. The first time it came out in a squeak. I cleared my throat and tried again. "Todd," I belted like I was calling out his food order in a busy cafeteria. He turned around looking rather startled.

"Hi!" I chirped cheerfully, as if we hadn't spent the entire evening in the same room.

"Hi," he said looking slightly bewildered.

I plunged ahead like a drowning woman. "I wanted to talk to you."

He looked a little like a deer caught in headlights, so I quickly added, "About your mission work. You see, I'm interested in missions."

"You?" he said in such a shocked tone that even I was a little daunted.

"Yes. I've done a lot of research on Nigeria. I'm especially interested in your work with AIDS patients. Could we talk about it sometime?"

He looked a little more interested and I relaxed. "Sure."

"Would you like to come to my place for dinner Saturday night?"

He pursed his lips in thought, making me want to plant a kiss on them right then and there. "I guess that could work," he said.

"Great, come to my place at seven o'clock. I'll write the address down for you." I took out a piece of paper and used my knee to write on, hoping he noticed the new skirt I'd bought to wear tonight. I was sure it made me look thinner. But when I looked up, he was looking at his watch as if anxious to get going. "See you then," I said with all the enthusiasm of a child looking forward to the circus.

He just nodded and turned to go. I watched him get into his car and drive off. He stopped for a moment to pet a dog that had wandered by. Yep, he was one dreamy guy.

5

Saturday morning I woke up so excited that I had trouble sitting still. I cleaned the apartment until it shone, even washing the curtains and vacuuming under the sofa. I went to the grocery store and bought the largest, most expensive steaks I could find. I had my hand on a bottle of champaign and then hesitated, not sure whether missionaries abstained from alcohol or not. I bought a bottle of sparking grape juice instead to be on the safe side. After adding two bouquets of fresh flowers to my cart, my spirits lifted even higher.

At home I set the table with my grandma's china that had been passed down to me. I put candles on the table and experimented with the lighting until it was just right, not too dark to see the food or too bright to ruin the atmosphere. I put books about Africa out that I'd just purchased and put some African music on in the background.

Finally, I put on a new dress that was perfect: modest, which would befit a missionary wife, but just enough on the flirty side to catch his attention. Then I let all caution go to the wind and put on a ton of perfume.

When my doorbell rang, I answered it only after the second ring. I opened the door with a little flour on my hands to show what a good cook I was. He stood there looking a little sheepish when he saw the candlelight, but when he heard the African music, he perked right up. He stepped in and made straight for the sofa to look at the books I had laid out.

As I worked in the kitchen, I kept peeking around the corner to catch a glimpse of him. In between things cooking, I sat on the sofa next to him while we pored over the books. The books had been a great idea. It got him talking.

"I've been to this market," he said as he pointed to a picture. "It's in Lagos, where I live. In fact, the owner and I are good friends." He smiled broadly which made him even better looking. I realized that I hadn't seen him smile very much, one more reason why he needed me. I was great at making people smile.

"Looking at these pictures makes me want to go there."

He glanced up at me as if noticing me for the first time. His direct gaze almost did me in. I once again fought the urge to throw my arms around his neck. "So when did you get interested in Nigeria?" he asked.

My daydreams shattered like so many shards of broken glass. I hadn't thought of an answer to that question. I jumped up like I'd been bitten. "Oh, almost forgot. I've got to check the potato casserole in the oven. I'll be right back."

I made a great amount of clanging in the kitchen to let him know I was indeed checking the casserole. Finally, I came back in. "Sorry about that. It wouldn't do to eat burnt potatoes. Anyway, in answer to your question, I think it has been since you've been sharing about it in our Bible Study. It has been fascinating to me and I can't learn enough about it now."

That seemed to please him. "Well, what do you want to know?"

"Everything."

He laughed. "That's more than I can tell. How about if I start with what daily life is like there?"

"Great."

"Well, I have to go to the market every day. The refrigerators are very small and the electricity is unreliable. I buy my chickens live because then I'm sure they're fresh."

"Live?"

"Yea."

"How do you eat them, then?"

"I have to cut their heads off and pluck them."

I hoped he didn't notice the horror that washed over my face. I couldn't imagine myself doing that in ten thousand years. Maybe I'd become a vegetarian. I'd leave the butchering to him. He went on without noticing my reaction. "Then I spend every weekday visiting AIDS patients in their homes. Many are receiving no treatment at all. At least I can bring them something to make them comfortable, read to them, and help take care of their children. I do a lot of cleaning, trying to keep the disease from spreading. Some of the patients live in real squalor."

"Oh, I imagined them in the hospital. I thought you visited them there."

"No, those patients are already being cared for. I spend my time with the ones who have no one to care for them."

I tried to picture myself cleaning and taking care of small children. I was having real trouble with the mental picture. Maybe I could just be a homemaker and spend some time tutoring. I decided to pursue that idea. "What are your living conditions like?"

"Oh, I live in an apartment about the size of this one. Another missionary lives with me. It's not as nice as this, though."

I took that as a compliment and was sure that Todd's apartment just needed me to fix it up. "Is Lagos a big city?"

Cherry Cobbler

"Huge. Nigeria is the most populated country in Africa."

"So, there are plenty of modern conveniences?"

"Not like here. We have electricity and running water, but it goes off half the time. Transportation isn't real reliable, so I walk a lot. Keeps me in shape."

I looked at him and agreed. He was certainly in shape. Maybe that's what I needed to get rid of my extra pounds. That made me think of food. I jumped up to check the dinner for real this time.

As we sat down to dinner, he prayed, "Thank you, God, for all this abundance. Amen." As he dug into his steak he said, "Wow, this is great. You're a good cook."

I smiled with satisfaction that he was noticing one of my better qualities. It was time to get more personal. "So, does it get lonely when you're on the field?"

He nodded as he struggled to swallow before he spoke. "It sure does. That's the toughest part, which is why I'm back here right now. I need to get my breath."

I took a breath and decided to go for broke. "Any romances back in Lagos?"

He laughed, "No. I wish there was. Just me and my roommate getting in each other's way."

I smiled and decided to plant a thought. "I guess you'd have to find someone who is willing to be a missionary."

"Exactly. There aren't too many women like that around."

I wanted to stand up and throw my arms out saying, "Here I am. I'll go." But even I knew that was over the top. So instead, I offered him a second helping of potatoes.

Cherry Cobbler

6

On Monday Mrs. Vanderweide blew in, appearing like a tornado that landed in our office. "Where is Mr. Hopkins?" she asked, loud enough to be heard in the next county. Today she had traded her fur for leather and her short skirt for a long, flowing silk that looked as if it belonged in Hawaii.

As I stammered that he was out, she focused on me. "What are you doing in that horrid foundation? I told you last time that it was not a good shade for you. You need more color. I can't help you if you don't listen to me." Her hands were on her hips and the only thing I could think of was that at least she had been distracted from Mr. Hopkins.

Before I could respond she blew back out. "I can't chase that man down forever," she said as she left. "I've been trying to call him all morning. Tell him to call me back right away. Evidently fifteen messages on his cell phone makes no difference to him. My pool has to be done by Saturday. I'm throwing a party."

I was pretty sure that Mrs. Vanderweide threw a party every Saturday night. I was also pretty sure that Mr.

Hopkins would get it done by then. Without Mrs. Vanderweide's business, we'd all get a pay cut.

Mr. Hopkins was an amazing landscape architect. He could solve almost any problem. I'm still astounded about how he took care of Mrs. Johnson's desire to have plants that didn't need water. He installed a pond and put plants around it that could nourish themselves from that constant water source. If anyone could keep Mrs. Vanderweide happy, he was the man.

He walked in a moment later. As I started to speak, he held his hand up. "I know. I saw her leave - actually rode around the block a couple of times to make sure she was gone. Believe me, I got her messages. I'm taking a crew over there this afternoon."

I nodded and smiled. I'd miss him an awful lot when I went to Africa. After Saturday night, I was pretty sure I'd be going. Todd and I had a great time. He even looked for me on Sunday. I told him that I'd be going to the soup kitchen on Saturday and he offered to join me. Yep, my plan was going perfectly. He'd see in no time that no one could be better for him than me.

There were a few times Saturday night that I worried that maybe things would be a little rough for me in Lagos. But then I reasoned that every man lives a little more Bohemian until a woman raises his standards. I was sure that is what would happen with us.

Cherry Cobbler

I'd wanted him to kiss me in the worst way on Saturday night, but he didn't seem to have a clue. Even when I reached up next to him when I was putting away the dishes, he failed to take advantage of my perfect position. Ah well, these things can't be rushed.

Wednesday night couldn't come soon enough. When I walked in, I felt comfortable sitting right next to Todd on the sofa. He talked to me like an old friend, and I felt a thrill go through me when his leg brushed up against mine. I left it there and invited Grant to sit on my other side so that we'd have to be squished together.

I hung on Todd's every word and agreed with everything he said. When the reading group ended, Grant started talking to me. I'd forgotten he was there. "You sure look pretty tonight, Cherry. You remind me of the cherry blossoms on the tree back home."

"Thanks, Grant," I said, annoyed that he was distracting me from Todd.

He pushed his glasses up his nose and ran a hand through his unruly hair. It didn't work. They both slid down again. "If I came in to the garden center sometime, would you help me pick out some houseplants?"

"I'm in the office. Someone in retail could help you." I turned away because I noticed that Todd was getting ready to leave. I had to follow him out.

We walked out to the car together and chatted for a few more minutes about the book we were studying. "Do you want me to pick you up Saturday to go to the soup kitchen?" he asked. "No use taking two cars."

"Sure."

"See you then."

He put his hat on his head and slid into the car making him look all the more like Indiana Jones. I stood on the sidewalk watching him drive away, sighing in contentment.

I turned to go to my own car when I ran smack dab into Grant, almost falling down. "Oh, I'm sorry, Cherry. Are you all right?" he asked as he helped steady me.

"Good grief, Grant. Why were you so close?" My voice sounded every bit as annoyed as I felt.

"I was just walking to my car. I didn't expect you to turn around so quickly." At that moment he looked down and his glasses slid right off his nose and hit the ground. I picked them up and shoved them on his face. "Why don't you get a new pair of glasses? And a haircut? A few new clothes might help too."

I felt a wee bit guilty when I saw his face fall. He was a nice guy, but someone needed to help him. I stomped off to my car and drove away like I was in the Indy 500.

7

Roslyn called the next day, "How about dinner at my place Saturday night?"

"I can't. Todd will probably ask me out. We're spending the morning together at the soup kitchen."

Her voice took on the same tone as my mother. "Now what makes you think he'll ask you out?"

"Because, Roslyn, we're getting along great. In no time he'll realize he can't live without me."

"Okay...but don't come crying to me when you're sitting alone on Saturday night."

"I promise."

"How about Friday night then? My parents are home that night, so I can't have you over, but we could go out."

"Sounds great. You're my second favorite date."

"Invite anyone else you want to come. Maybe even Todd. I need to meet this infamous young man." She said the last phrase as if she was quoting Shakespeare.

"No thanks. If I let him meet you, I'm sunk."

"What do you mean?"

"You're beautiful, and you have spent time overseas."

"Therefore, it follows that he'd fall madly in love with me." Her voice dripped sarcasm the way syrup drips off a pancake.

"It could happen. I'm not taking any chances."

"It seems if he thinks you're the one, he wouldn't be so easily swayed."

"He may not know I'm the one yet. I can't be too cautious at this stage."

"Very well, mon amie. See you Friday. I'll try to look extra dowdy to boost your self confidence for Saturday night."

"Thanks. You're a great friend."

"I know."

I hung up the phone and smiled. I loved that woman.

Saturday dawned bright and beautiful. Todd showed up right on time and played the gentleman by opening doors for me. I'd actually volunteered at the soup kitchen for a while in college, so I was in pretty comfortable territory. I was great with food and good with people, so I did well there.

Cherry Cobbler

Todd was wonderful too, of course. He treated everyone with dignity and joked around with the children. I was especially happy to see him interact with kids. If we had children, somebody would have to be good with them.

Afterwards, we ate leftovers as we sat outside on the hood of his car. He even put a blanket on it for me so I wouldn't get dirty. There was no doubt about it. We were getting along great. When I said I wanted to see a movie that night, he picked right up on it. We made a date for that evening.

I lived in euphoria that afternoon. I'd never been so sure that a man was right for me. I ran out and bought some new jeans and a peasant top that looked completely feminine. I spent a little more time on my hair and makeup than usual and found a lipstick shade that made my lips look full but not garish. Definitely not from Mrs. Vanderweide's line.

When my doorbell rang, I opened it slowly with what I perceived to be a sultry look on my face. But whatever expression I started out with, it quickly disintegrated into disappointment, if not downright annoyance. Todd stood there grinning, flanked by Grant and Josh. How did they get on my dream date? Todd let me know right up front.

"Hi, Cherry. I ran into these guys at the grocery store this afternoon. They said they hadn't seen this movie so I invited them along. The more the merrier, huh?"

I couldn't tell you what the movie was about. I divided my time between sneaking peaks at Todd and firing looks of murder at Grant and Josh. I tried to snuggle close to Todd and pretend we were the only ones there, but the theater was crowded and it was a comedy, so it was hard to get the right mood. When it was over, he dropped me off, saying he needed to get home and get some sleep. It had been a long day.

The next week at Bible Study, I got there early to make sure there was room on the sofa for Todd to sit next to me. But Mark and Sarah sat down beside me and Todd didn't come in until late so there was no way to make it happen. Grant didn't come at all which made me feel slightly guilty as I remembered how I treated him at the last Bible Study. But Josh said that Grant had to speak at a new AA chapter that was starting up, so I ceased worrying about it when I heard that.

I couldn't follow Todd out to his car, either, because I had to stay late to work on a drama that Jeannie and I were writing together. It made me sad to see him walking out without me. I belonged at his side.

While Jeannie cleaned up in the kitchen, Josh sat down next to me looking as if he knew a secret he was dying to tell. And such was the case.

"Cherry, Grant would kill me if he knew I was talking to you about this, but he's crazy about you."

Cherry Cobbler

I felt my heart sink right down to my toes. Maybe even lower. Grant was a nice guy and I hated breaking his heart. "What do you mean?" I asked like a stupid eighth-grader. What did I think he meant?

"He'd love to ask you out, but he's afraid you won't go. I figured that you just needed to know he was interested. I mean, Grant is the nicest guy in the world. What woman wouldn't want to date him?"

Indeed, I thought. I wanted to make Josh stop talking but he continued to rattle on. "He told me that he fell in love with you at first sight. That you're the most beautiful woman he's ever seen and that you've got the best personality. He said you could cheer up even a month of rainy days. He says you're the kind of woman worth waiting a lifetime for."

I really was speechless at these words. No man had ever said anything like that about me to my knowledge. If only it had been Todd saying them. I almost smiled but stopped myself. I had to nip this in the bud right now. "You know Josh, that's one of the nicest things I've ever heard, but Grant is right. I'm just not interested in a serious relationship with him."

Josh's face fell as if someone had erased his good nature and replaced it with an upside down smiley face. I'm sure he had some more words for me, but Jeannie came in, ending the conversation. Josh muttered something about forgetting everything he said, and then he melted out of the room like an ice cube on a 100-degree day.

Todd came to pick me up again for the soup kitchen. Saturdays became our day together. We worked together in the morning and often did something fun at night, although he almost always found others to go with us. He began to share with me deep concerns he had for his work back in Nigeria and talk a lot about visions for the future. I pictured myself in each scene that he painted.

He still hadn't kissed me, but he did give me a hug one night. I realized that he must be under a different standard than the rest of us since he had such a holy calling.

Meanwhile, it was the busy season at work. Everyone wanted their plantings done now. I began to work longer hours just to keep up, even filling in at retail once in a while when they were shorthanded. I figured I could use the overtime to pay for some extra luxuries in Nigeria.

Then it happened. I finally got the cold that everyone else had two weeks before. Because things were so hectic at work, I took as many drugs as I could and still stay conscious and went to work. Mr. Hopkins was the first to see me.

"Cherry, you look awful. You should be home in bed."

Cherry Cobbler

"Think about that a minute," I said as I held a tissue under my nose.

He nodded, "You're right. We couldn't spare you for a minute, but at least no overtime today."

"It's a deal."

Of course, the minute you get sick things get twice as busy. The phone rang and two people walked in simultaneously. While holding the phone with one hand and writing with the other, I tried to nod to the two new customers. My note was illegible because I also had to wipe my nose with my writing hand. So here I was, hunched over so that my nose touched the tissue in my hand as I scribbled. It must have been a lovely sight.

As soon as I hung up the phone, it rang again. The two new customers waited patiently. I'd finally gotten off the phone and turned my attention to them when Mrs. Vanderweide breezed in. Truly. Like a swift wind that not only ruffles your hair, but turns your umbrella inside out. Fortunately she just had a note for Mr. Hopkins. I was beginning to think she had a crush on him, as often as she came in.

The morning continued in this vein, with me alternately speaking on the phone and helping new customers. By noon I felt I'd been here a hundred years and wasn't even sure what I was saying.

One of the customers was an elderly African-American woman who'd been in before. She came in to complain because she'd called that morning and I'd disconnected her twice. She walked in looking like a thundercloud that was about to release a torrent. But after taking a glance at me, she turned into one of those soft, fluffy clouds you want to stretch out on. "Good heavens, child. You look awful. No wonder you kept disconnecting me."

"I'm sorry, Mrs. Murphy. I feel terrible that you had to come all the way here."

She sank down in a chair, "Well, I haven't got anything else to do. I actually came in to complain to you instead of going over your head. I wanted to give you a chance to make it right."

"Thanks, Mrs. Murphy. I'll try hard never to do it again."

"Well, you can't be responsible for what you do when you're sick," she said, looking me over as if I were a car she was going to buy. "Anybody doctoring you?"

"Just the local drug store."

"For heaven's sake, girl, you need help. I'll be back in a minute."

She left and I continued to answer the phone. About twenty minutes later she was back with a thermos, a china tea cup, and a sack of remedies. She piled everything on my desk and made some honey lemon tea in that sweet little antique cup. She also gave me several vitamin C pills and some echinacea. Then she announced that she'd answer the phone while I took a break and sipped my tea.

"But, you won't know what to do."

"Sure I will, child. I was a secretary for forty years. I'm the best there is. Now you go sit over there and sip. Better yet, take a nap."

I went over to the waiting room chair and sat down while she answered the phone. I had to admit that she acted as if she'd been working here all those forty years. I started to relax and found myself dozing off.

When I awoke, an hour had passed and my desk was as clean as I'd ever seen it. Mrs. Murphy had everything organized. "Why Mrs. Murphy, I could kiss you."

She looked at me in a threatening way. "Don't you dare. I don't want what you got!" She stood up and gathered her things together. "Well, you'll make it through the day now. You just call me if you need me again. Mrs. Murphy will take care of you."

As I watched her walk away, I thought I'd like to take her with me to Africa.

8

The next day my cold was only slightly better but because of Mrs. Murphy's treatment, I felt new courage to face my day. I managed fine and don't think I hung up on anyone. I was just about to take my lunch break when Grant walked in. "Hi, Cherry. I just came in for some houseplants so I thought I'd drop in and say hi."

I was glad to see he didn't hold our last meeting against me or felt that our friendship was over because of what I'd told Josh. "I'm just taking my lunch break."

"Oh, I don't mean to bother you."

"No bother. You want to sit with me while I eat? I'll warn you, though, I've got a cold."

"I could tell you didn't feel good. I had that cold a few weeks ago. It won't bother me. It's a bad one though, isn't it?"

"I'll say. I was hoping I'd die yesterday."

We sat down outside since it was such a pleasant day. "What is it you do again, Grant?"

Cherry Cobbler

"I'm a teacher - history - at the local high school. I love working with students."

"Do they listen?"

"Some do, some don't. If I can get one that doesn't to pay attention, I feel like I've done a lot."

"I have a teaching degree, but I can't stand it. I can't keep order."

"You have to focus on the individual student rather than the whole class or you'll get discouraged. I just hope I can reach one kid in a year; that at least one student will learn to love history or get interested in school because I was their teacher."

"That's nice." I didn't really know what to say next or care whether the conversation continued at all. "Did you find some houseplants?"

"I did. I've wanted some for a while. A really helpful woman showed me some that don't take too much care. I'd hate to kill them." He looked around. "This must be a great place to work - to be around growing things all the time."

"Yea, I guess." I looked around. It was a nice environment to come to every day. Grant seemed to appreciate the little things in life. It did me good to be around him. I was always dreaming of the exotic future while he seemed content to smell the roses in the here and now. His presence calmed me somehow.

"You seem like the kind of woman who should be surrounded by blooming things." He looked at me in a way that made me uncomfortable. He obviously read my feelings. "Well, I've got to get back to work. I'm on my lunch break too." He stood up with a smile and sauntered off. I was relieved to see him go. I wish Todd would make his intentions known so that I didn't have to ward off people like Grant.

Two days later it was my birthday. It pained me to be turning twenty-nine. It seems as if no one believes you when you really turn twenty-nine. They all think you're in your thirties and just saying that. It was rather awful to think of leaving my twenties anyway. Maybe if I were married it wouldn't seem so final.

All day I moped around. No one remembered at work, which suited me fine. I didn't really want any reminders. When the day finally ended, I headed home to a quiet evening. I'd hinted to Todd that it was my birthday, and he told me to have a good one. I was disappointed that he didn't want to take me out.

I trudged into the apartment and put my purse and jacket on the chair. I'd just slipped my shoes off when a mob of people came out of my bedroom. I jumped like a grasshopper, I was so startled. Roslyn, Jeannie, Sarah,

Cherry Cobbler

Megan, the women from work and even Mrs. Murphy (I'd told Roslyn about her) all surprised me. "How did you get in?" I asked, bewildered.

"Don't you remember?" Jeannie said. "You gave me a key to water your plants when you went on vacation two years ago. I just never gave it back." She stood there smiling in her beautiful blond perfection and I couldn't hold that against her for a moment. She was a great friend.

"We thought you needed an all girls' night," she went on. "So we've planned for a massage therapist to come over. She's actually my friend Marcie, who is in massage therapy school and we count as guinea pigs for her class."

"And I got Mrs. Vanderweide to donate a bunch of finger nail polish so we can give each other manicures and pedicures." Lucy was in retail at the garden center and one of my favorites there.

"And best of all," added Roslyn with a swing of her arms, "we've got three different chick flicks to watch while we do it all."

"Plus my homemade birthday cake and ice cream," Mrs. Murphy added with a smile. "I can see my remedies worked. You're looking much better, Miss Cherry."

"I sure am," I said as I gave her the hug I couldn't give her a few days ago. "You all are the best."

And it was my best birthday yet. We put on music and danced around while waiting our turn with the massage lady. Mrs. Murphy had brought some Ella Fitzgerald CDs and she belted out the tunes along with it as we swayed to the beat. Lucy did my nails in siren red under orders from Mrs. Vanderweide (the only reason she would give us the polish), and we experimented with some wild hairstyles. Mine ended in a punk style that stood up straight on my head, complete with pink hair spray. Roslyn took pictures to commemorate the occasion.

Just as I lay down on the massage bed, my door burst open. In walked a young woman with long black hair teased to three times its normal size, black makeup smudged around her eyes making her look a bit like a raccoon, and jeans as tight as a snake's skin. She looked around the room until she focused on me then yelled, "I hate your brother!"

9

Only Roslyn and I knew who she was. True to form, she trotted into the room, oblivious to the fact there was a party going on and said, "He's left me for another woman." Then she put her head down and bawled like Lucy in an "I Love Lucy" episode.

I resisted the temptation to tell her to leave my party. Instead, I got up from the massage table and went to sit next to her. Roslyn rolled her eyes at me. She'd had the pleasure of Crystal's company more than she ever wanted when we were roommates. Back then we hoped against hope that my brother would come to his senses and marry someone else, but we had no such luck. What he saw in her I'll never know.

"Why don't we go in my bedroom, Crystal? We can talk there."

She looked around the room as if noticing for the first time that there were other people here. She nodded in such a pitiful way that I actually felt a bit sorry for her.

I told everyone to keep up the party atmosphere and we disappeared into the bedroom. Just as we sat on the bed, she popped up as if she'd been bitten. "Oh, I forgot Twiggy."

"You brought your cat?" I asked trying to decide whether to be annoyed or amazed.

"I had to," she wailed. "Twiggy's the only one that loves me." Then she ran out as if she needed to rescue the cat from a fire.

A minute later she was back with her ugly, hissing, mournful sounding Siamese cat. It was yowling like it had its tail caught in a vice. "What's wrong with her?" I asked without concealing my distaste.

Crystal hugged the cat to her ample bosom making Twiggy's whining sound like a muted siren. "She's upset because I am. We understand each other."

I looked at the cat and doubted it very much. That creature looked like it only understood fish and chicken. I felt it best to keep the subject off of Twiggy, well named because it looked either like a starved super model or a bunch of sticks glued together. "So, you want to talk about what happened?"

Before she could say a word, a peal of laughter came from the living room. It set her off, "How could you have all these people over when I'm in such a crisis?"

Resisting the urge to pull out half of her too-abundant hair, I said softly and deliberately, enunciating each syllable as if I was talking to a two-year-old. "I didn't know you were in crisis, now did I?"

"Well, I am," she announced as if the world revolved around her and everyone should automatically know when she was distressed.

"Out with it." I was done being gentle.

The tears started again in earnest. "Sam left me for another woman." This came out in a squeak, like it was too incredible to be believed.

"Who?"

"Some woman he works with who wears business suits twenty-four hours a day," she snorted. "How could he leave me for that type? I could understand it if she wore leather pants or something."

I imagined that my brother finally came to his senses. Too bad it came so late. "So he wants a divorce?"

"I don't know!"

"You don't know? Then who does? The neighbors?" I knew I should be nicer but I just didn't feel like it. She didn't seem to notice. I think I could have stood on my head and she wouldn't have noticed.

"I caught him with her at a restaurant. We didn't talk about it."

"Maybe it was a business dinner."

She looked at me like I'd grown two heads. "One does not have a business dinner gazing into each other's eyes and holding each other's hands. They looked like they were ready to start making love any minute." The thought caused her to squeeze Twiggy until she squeaked. I almost felt sorry for the pitiful little animal.

"Well, you've got to go back and talk to him. You need the story from him. Appearances can be deceiving, and maybe he's sorry."

She looked like a rabbit staring down the barrel of a shotgun, "I can't," she whined. "I can't face him right now. Twiggy and I will just stay here until we can think clearly." The cat was starting to claw her way over Crystal's shoulder. Twiggy seemed to be thinking clearly enough.

"I don't think it will work out, Crystal. I only have one bedroom."

"That's okay. It's a double bed. We can share." Without another word she left the apartment after handing me Twiggy, who promptly jumped down and hid under the bed. To my dread she brought in a suitcase big enough to hold clothes for a couple of weeks. My heart sunk but rather than make a scene in front of all my friends, I let it go.

Cherry Cobbler

Mrs. Murphy grabbed my arm and told me to finish my massage, "You're going to need it, girl," she added with a nod toward Crystal.

A few minutes later Crystal was back in the room, joining the fun, all thought of my brother evidently flown from her mind. She was dancing, fixing everyone's hair, and telling jokes that kept us roaring. Even I was laughing which made me remember why my brother had fallen in love with her in the first place.

10

I'd been dreading going to work the next day but when I woke up and saw Crystal sleeping next to me in her leopard print pajamas, I sighed with relief that I didn't have to hang around my apartment that day. I quickly showered and dressed, grabbing a bite to eat on the run when my phone rang. I answered it quickly in fear that it would wake Sleeping Beauty.

"Cherry, is Crystal there?"

"Yes, Sam," I whispered hoping against hope that she wouldn't hear.

"You got laryngitis or somethin'?"

"No, she's sleeping."

"Well, wake her up. I need to talk to her."

I sighed loudly, "Is it true that you're cheating on her?"

"Not exactly." His voice went down two octaves and he sounded like a little boy who was being scolded by his mother.

"Not exactly?"

Cherry Cobbler

"It's complicated."

"I'm real bright - try me."

"I have to admit, I've been getting to know Kim. She's real nice. But we've never had more than dinner together. Nothing physical yet."

"I don't think Crystal's going to take that as real good news."

"Well, it's the best I've got."

Suddenly Crystal's voice came thundering through my small apartment. "Take what as good news?"

I held the phone out. "Sam wants to talk to you."

"Well, I don't want to talk to him."

"Aw, come on Crystal. You've got to talk to him."

"I do not. If he's going to cheat on me, I don't owe him anything."

I walked over and put the phone in her hand. "Then you tell him."

She looked at me with her eyes narrowed and her neck stuck forward. If she'd been a snake, I'd say she was about to strike, but she grabbed the phone and yelled, "Drop dead!" and then hung up. Great communicators, those two.

I threw my hands up in the air and then picked up my purse. "I'd suggest calling him back. You are not staying at my place permanently."

She stuck her nose up in the air as if sniffing for rain, "Not until he begs."

"Oh brother," I said, then walked out, literally praying for my brother.

As I drove to work, I thought about Crystal. I think one reason she annoys me so much is that I feel I could be just like her if I let myself go. It's a frightening thing to see all your worst qualities magnified for all the world to see. Another part of me loved her total confidence that Sam would come begging. To believe a man loved you so much that he'd beg to get you back was beyond my imagination. It almost made me root for her.

I'd been at work about thirty minutes when Sam burst through the door. "Cherry, she won't let me in!"

I looked at him suspiciously, "Shouldn't you be at work?"

"Yea, well some things are more important than work."

Wow, if I could just find a man like him. "Maybe you should have thought of that before mooning over Karen."

"It's Kim. And what kind of person says 'mooning over'?"

Cherry Cobbler

"Don't change the subject."

He sat down looking like a balloon that had a slow leak. "I know. It was stupid."

"So you don't love her?"

"Who?"

"Kim!"

"Kim? How could I love Kim when I've got somebody like Crystal?"

The question to end all questions, I'm sure. "So what was this Kim thing about?"

Sam looked miserable. He looked like someone had shot his only puppy. "I don't know." He twisted his hands until he caused them physical pain, as if punishing himself. "She's real nice, and she kept flirting with me. It kind of went to my head."

I started to say something else, but he interrupted. "But then Crystal walked in and saw us and I knew how stupid I was being. If Crystal left me, I don't know what I'd do."

"Well, she has left you, and she's driving me crazy."

"I don't know what to do," he whined, like he used to when we were kids.

"It seems she wants some begging."

"Aw, I don't want to beg," he continued to whine, as if accepting the inevitable.

"Look, Sam. You've wounded her ego something terrible, believe it or not. I think she wants to believe that you are still madly in love with her. Prove it to her, and she'll come back to you."

Sam brightened like a light bulb had been turned on inside of him. "All right, I can do that! Thanks Cherry, you're the greatest," and he came over and clasped me in a bear hug.

A minute later I got back to work, wondering what in the world he intended to do.

I found out when I got home that evening. My apartment was covered in flowers. There were bouquets on the coffee table, the dining table, the kitchen cabinet, the nightstands, the bathroom and deck. Baskets of chocolate covered every other square inch of the place. Crystal sat in the middle of all of it, stroking Twiggy and looking like she'd swallowed the canary herself. "He loves me," she said grinning. "Every single thing came with a note asking me to forgive him and telling me that I'm the only woman for him. Isn't he wonderful?"

I looked around and had to agree. He was either wonderful or completely insane. "So you guys talked?"

"Of course not," she said as if it was perfectly clear. "This is just stage one. In stage two I'll start answering his phone calls."

"He's been calling?"

"About every half hour today."

"And you never answered?"

"Of course not. Then he'd think I'm just waiting for him."

"Aren't you?"

"Sure, but he doesn't need to know that."

I shook my head. "Well, I'll see what leftovers we have for dinner."

"Nope. I'm taking you out. Sam will see that if he ever does anything like this again, it's going to cost him plenty. I bought three new outfits today." She stood up and modeled the new leopard print she was wearing. "So, where do you want to go?"

11

When Todd came to pick me up Saturday morning, I couldn't have been happier. Seeing those homeless people lifted my spirits. After living in wanton abandon for a few days, I was ready for the gritty reality of the street.

The worst part was introducing Todd to Crystal. It was like introducing Billy Graham to Lady Gaga. It made an odd picture. I realized that if I married Todd, we'd have to go to Africa. He'd never be able to put up with my family.

"So why's your brother's wife staying with you?"

"It's a long story."

"I see."

And we left it at that, which was best.

That evening we had our usual dinner and movie date, with only one other person there who had to leave early. I was sure he'd kiss me that night, but to my disappointment he shook my hand when he dropped me off. What was with that?

Cherry Cobbler

I found out on Wednesday. After Bible Study had ended, Todd announced that he was returning to Africa. My face must have dropped to the floor. I was stunned. I couldn't believe that he hadn't mentioned it to me. I sat there in a daze as people chatted around me. Finally as others packed up to leave, Todd whispered to me. "Can we go out for a coke? There's something I'd like to ask you."

My heart started racing and a goofy smile broke out on my face. Of course, he was saving the best for last. It was right here waiting for him all the time.

We drove in silence to a nearby coffee house and sat at a table in the corner. Todd looked nervous which I took as a good sign. "Cherry, there's something I've been wanting to ask you."

"Yes, Todd?" I leaned forward looking as available as I possibly could.

"You are obviously interested in missions in Africa."

I nodded to encourage him. "Yes, I am."

"Well, we need a woman on our staff there. Would you consider joining us?"

I thought it was a roundabout way to make a proposal but then again, any way was all right with me. I smiled slyly. "Todd, are you asking me to marry you?"

As soon as I said it I knew I'd made a horrendous mistake. Todd's face looked like someone had just punched him in the stomach. "No!" Then as the shock wore off, he started laughing. "Oh, you are such a kidder," he said shaking his head. "For a minute I thought you were serious. I always forget what a quirky sense of humor you have."

I laughed too, in a nervous, hysterical kind of way. My only thought was that I had to get out of here now before I lost it. "You know Todd, I drank way too much at Bible Study. I've got to go to the ladies' room." I jumped up like a greyhound running a race and bolted to the bathroom. I'd barely made it inside when the tears came in buckets. Fortunately, it was a one-stall bathroom because I was wailing. But as I cried, I saw all too clearly that everything I'd worked up in my mind to convince myself that Todd loved me had been completely misread. All along he saw me as a colleague, not a lover. The truth seemed as clear as the nose on my face, which actually looked rather blurry at the moment since my eyes were so watery.

I pulled myself together, reapplied some makeup and went back out. Todd hadn't a clue, as usual. "So, what do you think, Cherry? Will you come?"

I gave him the first truly honest answer since I'd met him. "I don't think so, Todd. I believe the one thing I've learned from knowing you is that I'd make a lousy missionary."

"But you're so good at the soup kitchen."

Cherry Cobbler

"Yea, but I get to go back to my comfortable apartment at the end of the day and watch my favorite movies. I'd just be a drag to you rather than a help."

He frowned but finally nodded. "Okay, I just thought I'd ask you. We really do need a woman there."

"I'm sure you do. Would you take me back to my car now?"

"Sure."

After another silent ride Todd said, "Well, it's been nice knowing you Cherry. I'll miss working with you."

"Yea, me too. Good bye, Todd." And with those final words, all my dreams of the future evaporated like a rain shower in the desert.

I walked into my apartment, forgetting for a moment all the flowers and perfume that would greet me. I'll have to say, though, Crystal was there for me. "Cherry! What happened to you? You look like you lost your best friend."

That's all it took. The tears started again. Crystal walked over without a word and pulled me over to the sofa. When I sat down, she put her arms around me and pulled my head down to her shoulder. "Go ahead and cry, honey. I'll be here to talk when you're ready."

It was nice. It was nice to come home to someone who cared about how I felt. It was nice to be hugged and comforted. It was nice to have someone who seemed to understand. So I finally quit crying and poured out my ridiculous story. Crystal was the perfect person to tell. "Oh, you poor thing. Men are so dense. That man has no excuse for not seeing that you were falling for him."

"But I'm the stupid one, Crystal. He never even kissed me and I made up all this stuff in my head about how he loved me."

"Well of course you did, baby. That's what we do. We are women, after all." Even though her words were perfectly illogical, I found them comforting somehow. It was awfully nice to sweep all my stupidity away with the excuse that I was a woman.

"I tell you what. I made lemon pie and rented a movie. I already watched it, but we'll watch it again together. It'll cheer you right up." She hopped up and I noticed she had another new outfit on. She was just now at the stage of answering Sam's phone calls, but would only talk to him for about a minute so of course, nothing had been worked out. I could never live with the drama she creates all the time, but she had it choreographed like a ballet. At the moment, I didn't care. She fed me and cooed over me and I didn't even mind when she plopped Twiggy on my lap. I felt loved and cared for which is all I wanted right now.

12

The next week at Bible Study I looked around the room and despaired. How was I ever going to meet anyone? I'd be lonely my whole life.

In retrospect, I realized that I'd have made a terrible wife for Todd, which depressed me even more. I wanted to be married so badly that I had begun to lie to myself about who I was. It made matrimony seem even more impossible.

What was worse, Crystal was gone and I actually missed her. My apartment was devoid of flowers and flamboyance and even of a furtive, mewing cat. Sam had finally managed to have a whole conversation with Crystal that actually lasted for two hours. He apologized for his behavior and promised to never do it again. She forgave him with a flourish and I thought at first I'd have to rent a room and give my apartment to them for the night since they were at each other like jungle animals. But they finally left with huge smiles on their faces, looking like honeymooners who'd discovered each other for the first time. I was enormously jealous.

At work a few days later, Grant once again dropped by. "Hey, Cherry. Did I time it right to hit your lunch break?"

"Sorry Grant, I took it early. My stomach was growling." I didn't mention that I always eat when I'm depressed.

"Okay, I just thought I'd ask."

"Back for more houseplants?"

"No, I like to come here on my lunch break. I love being outdoors and the weather is perfect right now. Nothin' like being in a garden on a seventy-degree day."

"You're right. It's a great place for lunch and so close to the school. Handy for you. Well, I've got to get back to work." I was hoping he'd take the hint, but he seemed all the more determined to stay.

"Uh, Cherry?"

"Yes?" I answered abruptly, the way a schoolteacher would answer a naughty child who kept bothering her.

"I just want to say..." He pushed his glasses back up and looked around the room as if groping for a clue as to what he wanted to say.

"What is it, Grant?" I knew I should make my tone softer, but I did have a lot of work to do.

Cherry Cobbler

Grant took a deep breath and plunged ahead, "I know that you liked Todd, and I wanted you to know that I'm sorry it didn't work out between you."

My eyes must have gotten two sizes bigger and my face had to be the color of Mrs. Vanderweide's favorite lipstick. "What makes you think that?" I really wanted to know. If Todd couldn't figure it out, how did this history teacher know?

"It was written all over your face. The way you'd light up when he walked in the room." He looked uncomfortable for a moment then went on. "I don't say that to make you feel bad. I just want you to know that if you ever need to talk to someone about it, I'd be glad to."

All animosity toward him left. "Thanks, Grant. That's sweet."

He put his shoulders back and lifted his chin as if attempting to save his dignity. "I'm sorry to bother you, Cherry. Have a good day."

I watched him walk off and thought maybe he would be good to talk to sometime. Maybe that's what I needed—a man's perspective on things. Maybe I wouldn't be so ridiculous about my crushes if I bounced them off a man. I'd call him sometime, but not right away. I needed to wallow in my grief for a while.

Of course, I still had Roslyn. She'd been a real sport about the whole Todd fiasco. After all, she'd been through this kind of thing with me before. She sympathized and never once said, "I told you so." Bless her heart.

I'd wanted to talk to Jeannie about the whole thing, but it was too hard. How do you talk to a blond, size eight who's married to a lawyer about your boyfriend problems? It's simply not going to happen. But it was comforting to be with her anyway. She sincerely liked me and we had so many common interests that we had a million things to talk about even if Todd wasn't one of them. I thought it curious though, that Grant had picked up that I liked Todd and Jeannie hadn't. Life is interesting sometimes.

When I hit the weekend, I knew I had to do something different. Sitting alone in my apartment was not going to work and going to the soup kitchen held too many memories at the moment, so there was only one thing left. I needed to go home to my mother.

13

I walked into the house and smelled oatmeal cookies baking. Blessed Mom. She knew I was coming and baked me cookies to cheer me up. "Wow, Mom, how sweet!" I could almost hear music playing in the background, it was so perfect.

"Don't get any ideas, missy. These are for the church bake sale." The music screeched to a halt in my mind. Oh yea, this was real life. She turned around and raked her eyes over me as if she was the sergeant and I was the private. "Well, you look all right. You haven't put on any more weight and your eyes aren't red and puffy, so you must be sleeping and not crying all the time."

"How about a hug, Mom?" I put my arms around her and she hugged me like a faithful mother.

"I'm sorry that your heart got broken again, Cherry. You want me to try to fix you up with someone? You know, Edgar Martin just got divorced. He was always a nice boy."

Even she could see the terror in my eyes at the suggestion. "No thanks, Mom. I never liked Edgar even before he was divorced."

My mother frowned so hard her eyebrows touched. "I never could understand that. He's such a nice boy."

"To you, maybe. All I remember about Edgar is when he refused to pick me for his basketball team in eighth grade gym class."

"For heaven's sake, Cherry. It's about time to get over that. Besides, you can't blame him. You're lousy at basketball."

"Be that as it may, I don't want anything to do with Edgar."

"Well, sit down. Let's think. There's got to be somebody just right for you."

I sat down as ordered. "Mom, I didn't come home to brainstorm about eligible men. I just wanted to get away from reminders of Todd."

Her eyes took on that look of omniscience. "I knew it wasn't going to work right from the start."

I cocked my head and challenged her. "How could you know that? You never even met him."

Cherry Cobbler

She picked up the mixing spoon and shook it at me. "I don't care how much in love you are, Cherry. You'd never survive in Africa."

I sighed. I hated it that she was always right. "I know. I see that now. I talked myself into believing I could do it if I loved someone enough."

My mother stood up and poured a glass of milk and put out a plate of the forbidden cookies after all. "I thought I couldn't have these," I looked at her trying to hide a grin.

"Oh, you know me. I made plenty. Eat up. It will make you feel better." My mother's philosophy of life.

"Cherry…"

I looked up. She had that expression that meant she was going to say something really important.

"No one knows you better than me, honey, and you need a man who will love you with his whole heart no matter what; someone who's crazy about you and will rearrange his life to fit you in."

"What about someone I can look up to, follow anywhere? That's what attracted me to Todd, besides the fact that he's gorgeous."

"Of course he needs to be a man like that. But you've got to be able to see yourself fitting into his life, too. And most of all, Cherry, you've got to keep from falling in love until you know that he's in love with you."

I ran my fingers through my short hair and pulled as if removing some hairs would clear my head. "That's just it. I seem to always think men are in love with me when they're not at all. I don't think I'm any good at this."

"Aw Sweetie, it'll happen one day. All of a sudden you'll look up and think, 'This is it. He loves me and I love him and I'm crazy enough about him to follow him anywhere.'"

I looked up with my teeth gritted. "What if there isn't anyone out there for me? What if I have to go it alone?"

My mother raised her chin, summoning up centuries of ancestral pride. "Then you'll go it alone with finesse. You'll be the best single woman around, making me proud. You always make me proud, Cherry."

I took her hand and squeezed it. "Thanks, Mama. It's nice to know someone believes in me."

She self-consciously stood up, tackling the dishes and changing the subject. "So Sam and Crystal are back together?"

"Yep, she played him like a trumpet. Each note exactly when she wanted it."

"You know, I'm growing to like that girl. She can get him to behave in a way I never could."

I chuckled. "That's for sure. Do you know I felt jealous of them?"

Cherry Cobbler

She shook her head. "My goodness, you are desperate!"

When Dad came home he fussed over me, telling me that Todd must have been blind and dumb to let me get away. I could always count on Dad to make me feel terrific. We spent the evening watching TV and eating popcorn. As my parents finished each other's jokes and gave each other fond looks, I knew that was exactly what I was looking for in a relationship.

14

Back at work on Monday, I called my best friend. "Roslyn, will you do me a favor?"

"Anything."

"Next time I say I'm in love, just hit me. A slug right to the jaw should do it."

"All right! Permission to slug you. I love it!" Then her mood changed. I could tell it even over the phone without seeing her face. "Cherry, would you consider going to Romania with me? I could do it if you were there."

"What would I do?"

"There's a school there. You could teach." She said it hopefully, as if she didn't even know me.

"Yea, right!"

She laughed. "Oh yea, I don't know what I was thinking. Never mind. Let's go to a movie tonight."

"On a Monday night?"

"Yea, why not?"

Cherry Cobbler

"You're right. Why not? Let's do it."

That evening I had a quick dinner and then swung by to pick up Roslyn. She was dressed in jeans and a short jacket and looked as cute as a miniature super model. I wanted to hug her right there.

Going into the theater, we ran into Grant and Josh. Grant smiled so big his glasses stayed up for once. "Aren't we lucky? Who would imagine that we'd run into the two most beautiful women in town?"

I smiled but Roslyn beamed. She'd never met either of them before and I never thought to tell her about them. To my shock, I realized that she was attracted to Josh. They began talking right away and I was astonished to see that they looked adorable together. I'd never even thought about that as a possibility. Josh always seemed like an attachment to Grant. I never thought of him as a separate individual.

Then I remembered that Josh was a nurse. Of course. They could talk about medical things the rest of us had no clue about. After I got over the shock, I felt happy for Roslyn even though that meant I was stuck with Grant. I was so lost in my thoughts that I didn't realize for a moment that he was talking to me. All I heard was, "Would you, Cherry?"

"What?"

"Would you consider helping me with the speech I have to give to the national AA meeting? You are so good at drama, I'm sure you'd be great at speeches too. I have it written and feel that it's what I want to say, but I need help with the delivery."

I looked at him. AA again. But I couldn't see any reason not to help. "Sure."

He lit up as if I'd given him a Christmas present. "Thanks, Cherry. That's just what I need. How about this Saturday?"

"Saturday would be fine." Actually, I felt glad about that. It would keep me from thinking about Todd. Anything to keep busy was all right by me.

We went into the theater and settled down to watch the movie, a suspense that kept us on the edge of our seats. About a quarter of the way in, I became confused about what was going on. Normally I'd ask Roslyn but she was busy talking to Josh, ignoring me completely, so I was forced to ask Grant. "Why did he just say that? I thought he didn't know about it." He patiently explained to me what was going on, apparently not annoyed at all my questions. Usually I annoyed everyone during a movie.

As the credits rolled and I stood to stretch, Grant suggested we all go out for coffee. I was about to refuse when I caught Roslyn's face. Those little girl eyes and curls framing her face fairly begged me to accept, so I reluctantly agreed.

Sipping coffee around the table, our conversation mostly revolved around the movie. I was able to clear up some of the fuzzy parts and give my opinion of the main character. We then moved on to talking about Roslyn's time in Romania. Both Grant and Josh were fascinated, but I was bored. I'd heard all about it a thousand times before.

"Well, this has been fun, but I've got to get home. Some of us have to work tomorrow."

"Yea, I'm the carefree one right now," Roslyn said as she tossed her curls, looking as lighthearted as I'd ever seen her. "I guess I should be considerate of you poor working class people."

Josh laughed far more exuberantly than her comment warranted and I thought, "He has it bad." By the time we reached my car, they'd made another date for Wednesday - didn't even wait for the weekend. My, oh my.

As I drove Roslyn home, she gushed, "Why didn't you tell me about Josh? He's adorable!"

I looked at her as if she'd been taken over by aliens. Never in my life had I heard Roslyn talk about a guy like that. She always talked about the latest procedure for applying a cast, but she rarely talked about men at all.

Usually she just listened to me and rolled her eyes a lot as I went on about how great someone of the opposite sex was. This was a role reversal that I wasn't entirely comfortable with.

"You think so, huh?" Not very clever of me, but I couldn't think of anything else to say.

She looked at me as if I'd lost a nose or something. "Don't you? I mean, I've never met anyone like him."

Which just goes to show that beauty is in the eye of the beholder.

15

On Saturday, Grant came over with his speech. It was really quite good. I read it first and was impressed about how well he expressed himself. Then he gave it to me out loud and I was even more impressed. When he spoke, he commanded great respect. His shoulders went back a little straighter and his eyes grew more intense. He was extremely articulate and said things in such a way that I hung on every word.

As I watched him, I thought he was somewhat of a buried treasure and suddenly wanted to make a project of him. He had quite beautiful eyes behind those horrid glasses and his hair was nice and thick. A decent stylist could do wonders with it. And a new wardrobe would be easy enough. I got excited as I thought about it. I love any kind of makeover.

I was so lost in thought about the idea that I didn't realize that he'd ended. "What did you think, Cherry?"

"Great!"

"You mean it?" He seemed very pleased.

"Yea, I wouldn't change a thing."

"That makes me feel really confident. I value your opinion a lot, Cherry."

"Perfect opening," I thought.

"Well then, I do have a suggestion."

"What's that?"

"Would you let me help you work on a new look for the speech? I could help you pick out glasses and a suit, and I've got a hairstylist who could do wonders."

He looked a little sad, and I couldn't understand why. "Okay." He hung his head and his glasses slid down his nose. "I guess I'm not very good at that kind of thing."

"That's why I want to help. You've got some nice features, Grant. You just need to work on it a bit. Your speech is wonderful, so now we have to give you a look to match it." He nodded and seemed more depressed than ever at my words. What was wrong with the man? Didn't he realize he needed help? "How about next Saturday? You make an appointment with your eye doctor and I'll make an appointment with my hairstylist. Then we'll go shopping in between for a suit."

I looked all bright and happy, because I was, and he took the cue and smiled wanly.

Cherry Cobbler

The week flew by and Saturday arrived as usual. I called Grant and he'd make an eye appointment for ten o'clock, which worked out well for the two o'clock hair appointment. He still didn't seem too excited and he hadn't said much at Bible Study on Wednesday. Not that it mattered much to me. I just wanted to help him get his look together.

At the eye doctor I picked out five different pairs of glasses, all the latest style that would be an enormous improvement over the ones he had now. He only liked one of them, but it was the one I liked best too so I was glad. He looked better already just trying them on. It was a one-hour place, so we decided to go shopping and then come back to pick them up.

The suit was even more fun to pick out. I found a nice three-piece one that was fitted and brought out his broad shoulders and narrow waist. It fit like a glove and transformed him from his usual cotton shirts and jeans. Even he was pleased with the overall effect. Only the pants needed to be hemmed, so we left them there and decided to get some lunch.

After ordering Grant said, "So, how are you doing getting over Todd, Cherry?"

I sighed. "It's hard. He was exactly what I was looking for. I don't see how anyone else will measure up."

He squirmed in his chair, as if he'd sat on a pinecone. "What was it about Todd that you were attracted to?"

A subject I liked. "Well, first of all, his rugged good looks. But also the fact that he had great ideas about life and that he wanted to help people. I found that appealing."

Grant nodded. "Those are good qualities." He took a sip of his coke and added, "You won't have trouble finding someone else, Cherry."

"What makes you think that?"

He looked surprised, "Because you're so beautiful and you've got spunk. I would think you'd have men falling all over the place for you."

I looked at him suspiciously. "What about my weight?"

"What about it?"

"Aren't I a little plump?"

"No!" He looked shocked. "You're perfect. Who would want a little skinny stick of a woman?"

I rolled my eyes as I took a sip of Diet Coke. "Only most of the world from what I see in magazines."

He waved his hand as if slapping away all those images. "Those aren't real women. They're some made up fantasy. Besides, you've got them all beat."

I looked closer at what he was drinking, making sure he hadn't fallen off the wagon. "What about you? Any women in your life?"

He turned bright red but shook his head. "No, I'm afraid not."

"Well, when I get done with you, they'll be flocking to you. We'll have you on the cover of *GQ* in no time."

He laughed to be polite, but I could see his heart wasn't in it.

After lunch we picked up the glasses and the suit and headed to the hairstylist. He already looked a hundred times better in his new glasses. While we waited, we flipped through books trying to find the right style. After looking at maybe fifty pictures, he chose a simple style that would be easy to care for. He didn't have any patience with messing with his hair.

When the stylist was done, I was amazed. He looked downright handsome. He had a dark, smoky, Italian look that sent chills up and down my spine. Suddenly I noticed that his eyes were a kind of grayish blue that looked steely and strong. His hair looked good enough to run my fingers through but of course, I restrained myself. I wanted him to try on the suit too, but he thought that was a bit much. I couldn't stop looking at him. I'd created a masterpiece.

16

Grant wanted me to come with him to the national AA meeting where he would give his speech. "Since you worked so hard to make me look decent, you ought to be there to see the final result."

I was glad to do it. Not that I really wanted to be with a bunch of former alcoholics, but I'd be proud to be with Grant. The makeover had turned out so well that I couldn't wait to see how women reacted to him. Besides, it was an excuse to get a new dress.

When he picked me up, he raved about how wonderful I looked, but I couldn't say a thing. The man was drop dead gorgeous. My knees would have been weak if I'd forgotten that it was Grant standing next to me. The women would be flocking around him tonight and I couldn't wait to see it.

"It means a lot to me that you'd come with me to this. It will give me courage to look out and see you as I give the speech."

"Aw, that's sweet, Grant. But I'll bet you'll have so many women falling at your feet that you won't even notice me."

"That would never happen." He said it as if I'd insulted him rather than complimented him.

"So, are you nervous?"

"Not really. I've told my story lots of times. It's a privilege to be on this side of things and seeing good results in my life. I'm blessed."

I thought about that a minute. It was hard to imagine Grant as an alcoholic. I'd never really considered what he used to be like. Now he seemed like a solid rock kind of person who would never be irresponsible. Others, like Josh, looked up to him and wanted to be like him.

When we arrived, I was introduced to far more people than I could remember. After the first couple, I began to tune out their names, not even trying to keep them at the forefront of my mind. Many people raved about Grant to me, which confused me. I tried to explain that I was just a friend, but nobody really cared. They wanted to tell someone how inspiring Grant was and I was elected. Several people commented on his new look, but most treated him no different than usual. I was disappointed.

We sat with Josh and Roslyn. She looked absolutely smashing in a red evening gown complete with sequins, a look so opposite of her normal appearance that I couldn't quit commenting on it. Evidently dating Josh had made her feel reckless. Usually, she'd ward off my compliments like an annoyed bear swatting a honeybee, but tonight she reveled in it. Josh brought Roslyn's previously hidden feminine side to the surface, making her more beautiful than she already was.

I was glad she was there because it gave me someone to talk to, but just as at the movies, she was absorbed in Josh's every word so I made polite conversation with others at the table. Grant turned out to be quite a conversationalist. He was comfortable with the people he knew here and kept things lively. Without a doubt, he was feeling cheerful and I couldn't help but give myself a pat on the back that I'd helped.

After dinner, Grant was introduced to thunderous applause. He engaged the audience with some jokes and then gave his knockout speech, which was even better than when he'd practiced on me. When the program ended, women crowded around him just as I'd predicted. I couldn't even see him, there were so many lovely ladies vying for his attention. I giggled to myself at the sight. Yes, I was extremely happy with my work. Maybe he'd even invite me to the wedding.

When he'd finally talked to almost everyone in the place, we made our way out to the car. Josh and Roslyn had wanted us to join them for late night coffee, but I was exhausted and wanted to go home. At the door to my apartment, Grant thanked me again for joining him. "It meant more than you know to have you there tonight. You gave me courage."

Cherry Cobbler

He squeezed my hand and held my eyes a moment too long. It made me uncomfortable, so to counteract it I went into my joking mode. "Yea, well, I have that effect on people." Then I opened my door and stepped in, leaving him outside. "It was a lot of fun. Let me know if any of those women show up at your doorstep tonight, and I want a front row seat at your wedding."

I laughed heartily, but he kept a steady gaze on me that rattled me a bit, "Oh, you'll be right up front," was all he said as he brushed his knuckles against the side of my face, giving me chills. I frowned slightly as he turned to go. How could he agree with me and make it sound completely different? I shook off the funny feeling I had and took off my coat. At any rate, my mission was accomplished. I'd transformed the man for some other woman.

17

Roslyn took a job at the local hospital as an emergency room doctor. I knew it wasn't at all what she wanted. The reason she liked Romania so much was the relationships she developed with individuals. If she stayed in the states she'd want a family practice in a small town, so the only possible reason that she took this job was so she could stay close to Josh.

This realization made me feel a little better about myself. I wasn't the only one who made rash decisions where men were concerned. Okay, maybe emergency room doctor doesn't compare to missionary wife, but all the same, her fondest dreams were put aside for this one measly guy.

On a weekend when he was out of town, we went out for dinner. "Well, I'm sure glad Josh had this fishing trip planned. I thought I'd have to make an appointment to see you again."

Roslyn actually giggled. The times I'd seen her giggle were so rare that it caused my mouth to drop open. She noticed and scolded me. "Now, come on. I've been through this a million times with you and haven't made too much fun of you, have I?"

My eyebrows shot up. "Yes, you have, and I'm not about to let an opportunity like this go by."

She smiled. "Okay. Fair enough. I admit I'm being a bit of a school girl about this."

"I should say! Floating about ten feet off the ground."

"Oh Cherry, I was beginning to think this would never happen to me. I think this is it."

"The One," I said slowly, emphasizing each word.

"I think so. I've never felt this way about anyone. He's perfect for me."

"How so?"

"He's lighthearted and not threatened by my profession. He makes me laugh and helps me take myself less seriously. He thinks I'm beautiful and tells me so all the time. He understands the ups and downs of my work and is proud of the fact that I want to go back to Romania. He's a great dancer, and just looking at him makes my heart do somersaults. Is that enough, or should I go on?"

I held up my hand like a traffic cop. "No, please stop. I get the idea." I took a bite, chewed carefully, then said, "I've certainly never seen you become so smitten with anyone before. I have to admit, I think it's genuine."

She beamed. "Even though I don't know what 'smitten' means, I concur." She leaned over and grabbed my hand, "Oh Cherry, it seems too good to be true."

I squeezed back. "If anyone deserves it, you do. I'm happy for you, Roslyn."

She tackled a rather hard roll then asked, "Are you over Todd?"

I leaned back in my chair and looked at the waiter walking by as if he'd give me the answer. Suddenly, I knew. "You know, I am. I haven't thought about him for a couple of days. I think it finally sunk in that I'd made Todd someone I wanted him to be rather than someone he really was." I took another mouthful and spoke around the food. "I'm really good at that."

Roslyn laughed. "I'll say! You should write novels."

I shook my head. "Not me! I'd be terrified of ruining everyone's life in the story. I don't like playing God."

I found out why Roslyn liked Josh so much a few weeks later. The "foursome", as we began to call ourselves, decided to go to the zoo. Looking at the monkeys grooming each other, we began to mimic what we thought they were thinking. Grant was the best at this and had us all in stitches.

Cherry Cobbler

Just as he said, "Hey, you missed a spot. Get behind my left ear," we heard a woman scream. That's when we noticed a small child climbing the fence. Josh moved quicker than a cheetah. He climbed the fence faster than the monkeys could and snatched the little boy down as if he'd being doing that for years. Handing him to his grateful mother, we all sighed with relief as the child let out a wail that even startled the primates.

We all decided at that point to sit down and relax with a coke. "How'd you learn to respond so quickly in an emergency, Josh?"

Josh looked awkwardly into the distance. "I've had a lot of experience watching my little brothers."

Roslyn helped him out. "He has three younger brothers that he raised."

"You raised them?"

"Well, eventually. Our folks were killed in an automobile accident when I was nineteen. My brothers were ages thirteen to seventeen. They would have had to go to foster homes if I didn't take care of them, so they came to live with me. That's what caused me to quit drinking."

"How did you support them?" I was asking all the questions. Roslyn and Grant already knew about it.

"I worked at a hospital and went to school on weekends to get my CNA. We also got some government help. It was hardest on my youngest brother, but somehow they all pulled through. The usual teenage rebellion was gone because everyone had to work to make ends meet. We're still unusually close today."

"What are they doing now?"

"The middle two are both engineers and the youngest is in college studying to be a doctor. He'll outshine us all."

I glanced at Roslyn and saw the light shining in her eyes. She had seen in Josh what I'd missed—a man who sacrificed for others. "And you?"

"I've always wanted to be a doctor, too, and hope to still make it one of these days. But right now I have to get my baby brother through. I've managed to get my LPN degree, so I can make a decent enough wage to be some help. My other brothers are helping him, too. In another semester, he'll start his residency."

"Are you jealous of Roslyn?" Roslyn gave me a look that should have sent me running.

He put his arm around her and squeezed. "Are you kidding? She's my ideal woman – brave, smart, adventurous, and absolutely gorgeous."

I felt all warm inside looking at them, thinking for the first time that they were a perfect couple. "How did you and Grant get to know each other?"

"He's the one who invited me to AA."

Cherry Cobbler

"Were you friends?"

"No. We worked together at the hospital. Grant was working his way through school as a janitor."

I looked at Grant and he made a motion as if he were sweeping. "I was a darn good janitor, too," he grinned.

"Anyway," Josh continued, "during lunch one day, I admitted my fear of raising my brothers when I couldn't kick my drinking. He told me his story and we've been stuck together like glue ever since. I would never have made it without Grant."

That made me curious. "What is your story, Grant?"

"It's so sad. It'll make you cry," he said dramatically.

"Oh, stop it and spit it out."

The shine left his eyes, and the tone of his voice changed from jovial to serious. "Can I tell you another day? I'm in too good of a mood to talk about it now."

I nodded my head and felt bad that I'd taken the cheer out of his eyes. I also became curious as to what his story held. The man was becoming downright mysterious.

18

Now that Todd was gone, I started enjoying Bible Study a lot more. When I wasn't trying to impress someone I was able to get more out of the lesson. And the ball I got rolling with Grant's appearance seemed to be gathering momentum. I noticed lots of new items in his wardrobe and wondered if another woman was helping him. "Are you cheating on me?"

He looked rather shocked. "What?"

"Are you letting another woman help pick out your clothes?"

The surprise in his eyes melted into a warm puddle of affection. "No, Cherry," he said softly. "I'd never let anyone take your place."

I punched him in the arm to lighten him up. "Oh, I was just kidding. You're looking mighty spiffy these days."

"Spiffy?"

"Yea, you look great."

Cherry Cobbler

"Oh, good. I've been trying to pick up a few new things here and there. It had been a long time since I'd bought new clothes."

"Really?" I said rolling my eyes.

He laughed. "That bad, huh?"

"Worse."

"Well, thanks for setting me in the right direction."

"So, how many of those women from the banquet have thrown themselves at your feet?'

He grinned, "Quite a few, actually."

"I knew it! Have you found one you like yet?"

"Only one, and she's the one playing hard to get."

"Don't give up. Good things come to those who persist."

"That's good advice, Cherry. I intend to do just that. Would you like to go for coffee? Josh is picking up Roslyn."

"What a surprise. Sure, I'll go. I only have work tomorrow."

It was a great evening. Roslyn and Josh were more fun to watch than a romantic movie. They'd get lost in each other for minutes at a time, and Grant and I would try to get their attention. We felt that we were true comrades, putting up with lovesick friends we didn't recognize. After a while we forgot about them and talked to each other.

"So Grant, what's new at school?"

His jovial expression turned serious. "I've got a kid I'm worried about."

"What's wrong?"

"He's a cut-up kid, the kind who's always trying to entertain the whole class. I give him a platform whenever possible so he can get it out of his system."

"How do you do that?"

"I assign him projects that put him up front and let him present it any way he wants as long as he keeps it clean. He gives history a hilarious spin and the other kids love it."

"So why are you worried?"

"I'm pretty sure he's doing drugs."

"What happened?"

"Nothing big, just little things. He hasn't been turning in his assignments, his eyes are bloodshot all the time, he's running with a different crowd than he used to, and he doesn't really care about entertaining anymore."

Cherry Cobbler

"That sounds bad."

"It is."

"What are you going to do?"

"I've sent some notes home to his parents and they've met with his counselor. They're good people and just as worried as I am; well, more really. They have to live with him. I only have him an hour a day. I've also talked to him about my past and what a dead-end it is but of course he thinks it would never happen to him."

All of a sudden I saw Grant as a teenager, trying to fit in, escaping his circumstances by drinking. I had to admire him for overcoming such a trap. I wanted to encourage him now, but I wasn't sure how. "Don't give up on him. It took a while for you and look how great you turned out."

He tried to smile but his heart wasn't in it. "I won't give up, but he sure keeps me from sleeping at night. You know, I have eighty great kids I see everyday but none of them occupy my thoughts like this kid does."

I nodded and thought about my work. The worst I had to worry about was wearing makeup I didn't like. It made me wish I'd tried harder with the teaching thing although I had the feeling some people were cut out to be a teacher and some weren't. As sure as I was that I wasn't, I was sure that Grant was. I hoped those kids knew how lucky they were to have him.

"Tell me more about what you were like as a teenager."

"I was shy and quiet. I sat in the background always wishing I could get the attention of someone like you."

I looked up to see if he was kidding. Grant had a subtle sense of humor that threw me off guard. I wasn't always sure whether he was being straight with me or pulling my leg. I had to know. "What do you mean?"

"People like you seem to have all the fun in life. I've always thought that if I could be around someone like you, all the joy and happiness would rub off on me."

Grant was smiling but something about that statement made me sad. "Are you unhappy?"

He laughed hard at that. "No, I'm not sad. I'm quite content. I'm just happier when I'm around you."

I squirmed in my seat, but somehow the way he said it made me feel wonderful. I've always had the sneaky suspicion that I was just a little too loud, a little too boisterous, and a little too frank. The thought that someone actually liked being around me warmed my heart, but I couldn't let him see that. "Aw, that's what everyone says."

"I thought so." He smiled and I felt myself flush red. The amazing thing was I think he really believed it. I decided to change the subject quickly. Staring at him, the subject came up quite easily.

Cherry Cobbler

"So, has anyone noticed your new look?"

He grinned, "A few. My students tease me about it the way they would an older brother who finally entered this century."

"So you haven't had to fight off the girls yet?"

"Thankfully, no. I don't think I've got the charm to go with it. They still see me as a fusty old history teacher."

"Just as well."

"Definitely.

"What's your favorite period of history?"

I'd asked the right question. He looked as if he'd won the lottery. "The middle ages, without a doubt. Give me knights and sword fights any day and I'm content. I even belonged to a reenactment group that met on weekends and during the summer. I made my own armor and costume. I still have it, if you ever want to see it."

"Uh, no thanks. I'm a thoroughly modern girl. No knights in shining armor for me." I meant it as a joke, but his face fell. I seemed particularly good at ruining Grant's day. Fortunately, Josh and Roslyn got into the conversation and saved me.

"I don't know...his armor's pretty cool. I've tried it on more than once." Josh smiled. Roslyn leaned over and whispered, "I'd love to see you in armor." I thought I'd throw up.

19

Mrs. Vanderweide showed up right on schedule. It was Monday morning and she always entertained on the weekend, so Mondays brought her to our door like clockwork. Today, however, she looked more bizarre than usual. She had on a bright orange blouse that billowed around her in a cloud of silk. Underneath all that fabric were black leather pants that looked at least two sizes too small. She looked like a pumpkin stuck on a two licorice sticks.

But what was more surprising was that her makeup was running. She constantly assured me that her makeup line could withstand a hurricane, so I figured that meant that she'd been crying up a tsunami.

Staggering up to my desk, she gave a short pretense of having it together, which disintegrated as quickly as a sandcastle at high tide. "Cherry," she squeaked, like so many mice were stuck in her throat. She cleared it and tried again. "Cherry." This time it sounded like a bulldog had eaten the mouse. I actually jumped. "Would you..." And whatever was supposed to come next got lost in a torrent of tears. The hacking and choking that accompanied this deluge was reminiscent of a thunderstorm.

In spite of my wariness about getting involved, I dived in anyway. "Are you okay, Mrs. Vanderweide?"

She looked at me with sad puppy dog eyes, red framed in black from all that non-run mascara that was pooling around her eyelids. Her eyes almost matched her outfit. "How do you do it, Cherry?" she sputtered out, causing me to blink.

"Do what?"

"Handle being single? I mean, really, we're two of a kind."

I hoped my eyes didn't reflect the horror I felt. I did not like all this sisterhood she was imposing on me. "What do you mean?"

"Well," she whined, "we both are a little plump, neither of us are natural beauties—although we do okay with makeup—and each of us is a loser at love." She actually swooned a little after this last statement, melodramatic even in her distress.

I decided to get the subject off of me as quickly as possible. This conversation was headed nowhere good. "What happened, Mrs. Vanderweide?" I asked in my sweetest tone. I could be a good actress, too.

"Oh, you wouldn't understand."

Cherry Cobbler

So much for the sisterhood. "Okay," I replied a little too cheerfully. It didn't matter. She went on as if I'd said, "Try me."

She sighed deeply, creating a breeze that ruffled my hair. "You think a man is madly in love with you and then he just ups and leaves. You wouldn't understand the burden of being wealthy. You never know if a fellow is interested in you or your money."

My bet was that no one would like Mrs. Vanderweide for any reason except her money, but then I thought of Crystal and changed my mind. "Where did you meet this guy?"

"At one of my parties."

"See, there you go. Maybe you should try a neutral place to meet guys so they don't know how wealthy you are."

She brightened up at this suggestion, looking even stranger as she smiled with her raccoon eyes and smudged rouge. "That's a great idea, Cherry. Where do you suggest?"

I could only think of my mother and what she told me when I went away to college. "At church. That's the best place," I said confident that I was telling the truth.

Mrs. Vanderweide's eyes got wide. "At church?" she said, looking like I'd suggested going to Jupiter. "I don't go to church," she said softly as if weighing such an outlandish thought. "What church?"

"You could come to mine. I'll even pick you up on Sunday."

"You'd do that for me?" She looked as humble and touched as I'd ever seen her. Then I thought about what I was advising.

"Sure, but of course, I can't guarantee you will meet someone. It could take a while."

"Well, I'm a patient person. I'll give it a couple of weeks." She seemed completely restored now which made me think she hadn't been in love with this guy but was only wounded by his rejection, which I knew a little bit about. I wondered if I'd done a bad thing. Is it okay to get someone to come to church through the lure of a mate? And who would realistically have anything to do with Mrs. Vanderweide? Oh well, I'd let God sort that out. I'd done my part.

"Okay, I'll see Mr. Hopkins now." And life at the office returned to normal.

When Sunday morning dawned, I had a vague notion to call Mrs. Vanderweide with pleas of a headache, but instead I dutifully pulled up to her mansion that was every bit as ostentatious as her clothes. I'd never seen a dwelling with so many turrets. It looked like a castle that had been designed by someone in Lego land. The real clincher was the pink and turquoise trim.

I'd just pushed the doorbell when Mrs. Vanderweide burst through the door. To my shock, she was dressed fairly conservatively. She had on a white linen dress, complete with a broad brimmed hat. She actually looked quite smashing. I told her so, and she beamed. "Yes, I haven't worn this since I went to the races. I think it works quite well for church, don't you?"

"Absolutely."

On the way there she peppered me with questions about available men. My heart started to sink until I thought of an answer. "If you want to impress anyone at church, you are going to have to act interested in what's going on there, not just in the men."

She looked a bit crestfallen. "I hadn't thought of that. I haven't been to church since I was ten. I don't even know what it's about."

"Well, maybe you should concentrate on that first," I gently suggested.

With that she sunk into an uneasy silence, looking worried.

When we arrived, all trepidation disappeared. Mrs. Vanderweide was in her element whenever people were around. She began greeting everyone as soon as she walked through the door. Most regulars didn't greet newcomers as well as she greeted them. She was all smiles and charm. It was a completely different side of her that I'd never seen before.

After meeting at least fifty people, she settled into a chair and looked around expectantly. A casual observer might have thought she was anticipating the service, but I knew she was scoping out the men. Her gaze finally settled on a distinguished looking older gentleman a few rows over. She smiled and focused her attention on the front.

When the worship band began playing, she looked pleasantly surprised. She leaned over and whispered, "This is a lot better than I remember church being. The last one I went to had organ music."

I nodded and smiled. She didn't know the songs but she tried to sing anyway, and loved swaying to the music. I worried for a minute that she might burst into dance and head out into the aisle, but she contained herself.

As the pastor got up I squirmed a bit, hoping Mrs. Vanderweide would really listen. She did. Attentively. I had no idea Mrs. Vanderweide could sit still so long. When the service was over, I started to ask her what she thought but she disappeared to our right, meeting

Cherry Cobbler

everyone she could as she worked her way over to the man she had her eye on.

I lost track of her after that, talking to Jeannie about an upcoming drama we'd be working on. Finally, after almost everyone had disappeared, she popped back at my side. "I won't need you to give me a ride home, Cherry. Mr. Finster is taking me to lunch." She leaned over and whispered, "This church stuff really works." Then she walked away, her wide hat bobbing with her energetic step.

20

I went home depressed. Mrs. Vanderweide had managed in one morning what I hadn't been able to do in all these years. Maybe I should consider wearing leather. I sighed and took out a carton of Rocky Road ice cream, making it my noon meal.

After polishing it off and tossing the carton in the trash (not only is it a great meal but clean up is a cinch), the phone rang. I snatched it up, surprised to hear Mrs. Murphy's voice. "Cherry, how're you doing this fine Sunday?"

"I'm okay," I whined like a little kid.

"You don't sound so good. You coming down with another cold?"

I cleared my voice and determined to sound perkier. "No, I'm fine, Mrs. Murphy."

"Good, because I fixed a huge meal for my daughter and she couldn't come at the last minute. Will you come over and help me with all this food and give me some company besides?"

Cherry Cobbler

I groaned inwardly at all that ice cream sitting in my stomach, but I answered cheerily, "Sure, Mrs. Murphy. How nice of you to think of me."

"I like your company, Cherry."

"I like yours too." I smiled, meaning every word.

"See you in a few minutes?"

"You bet."

I hung up the phone, grabbed my purse, and headed for the local grocery store. There I bought the best bouquet of flowers I could find. In less than ten minutes I was at her door. Mrs. Murphy lives in a sweet little cottage surrounded by all sorts of blooming things. She has them arranged just right without the help of any of our designers and makes sure every plant is pruned to perfection. I looked at the bouquet in my hand and despaired.

However, before I could even ring her doorbell, she threw open the door and exclaimed as if I was informing her that she'd won the Publisher Clearing House Sweepstakes, "Why Cherry! How sweet of you! No one has brought me flowers in a stone's age." She reached for them with her work-worn hands that were lovelier than any hand model's in a magazine. I just smiled like a bloomin' idiot. Her gratefulness felt like a medal of honor.

The inside of Mrs. Murphy's cottage bloomed as profusely as the outside. Not only did she have floral arrangements everywhere that made mine look ridiculous, but the whole décor blossomed. Chintz fabric covered the furniture and windows, making me feel like I'd been planted in a garden. I loved Mrs. Murphy.

"Do you like fried chicken, child?"

"I love it. It smells heavenly."

"It is. I make the best fried chicken this side of Georgia."

"I absolutely believe you."

"That's why I like you. You've got good judgment."

I let that bit of fabrication go and sat down at her lovely table, complete with lace tablecloth, candelabras, fine china, and crystal. I hadn't eaten so elegantly since my cousin's wedding. And I found out she wasn't exaggerating about being the best. "This is amazing chicken."

"Told you."

We ate companionably and I really wished I hadn't eaten that ice cream. "So what happened to your daughter?"

Mrs. Murphy sniffed. "She got a date after church. She loves me, but not enough to turn down a date."

"Wow, the church thing works for everyone but me."

Cherry Cobbler

"You thinkin' of leaving the faith?"

I laughed. "No. I'll keep going until I die, even if I never do get a date."

"Ah, I see. Some of your friends getting dates at church?"

I nodded, unable to talk with my mouth full of mashed potatoes.

"But not you?"

I shook my head, stuffing a big bite of bread in it, choosing not to talk. Mrs. Murphy didn't let me get away with that, waiting patiently for me to swallow. I finally did, took a drink, and wailed, "Mrs. Vanderweide had a date today. Her first time ever at church!"

"That's what's botherin' you?"

I nodded.

"Don't waste your time thinking about that, child. If Mrs. Vanderweide has forty dates, she can't hold a candle to you."

I just looked at her like she was speaking Chinese.

She put her fork down and ticked off her reasons. "One, you're pleasant to be around. Mrs. Vanderweide drives everyone batty in one easy lesson. Two, you're twice as pretty as she is." When I raised my eyebrows, she became as tenacious as a bull. "Yes, you are. Don't you go contradicting me," she said, as if I was arguing. "Three, you're right with God. Mrs. Vanderweide has a long way to go in that department. And even if you didn't have the first two things going for you that would be enough."

I smiled and actually got up and hugged her. "You're right. Boy, am I glad you called me today and that your daughter cancelled on you. You put me right back on track and I'll try to stay there for at least a day."

She grinned too, "Eat your chicken."

It was a good thing that Mrs. Murphy lectured me on Sunday, because on Monday Mrs. Vanderweide stopped in, gushing, "Oh Cherry, you we're so right. This man is great. He has no idea I have money and he came to church to meet good women too. It was his first Sunday also. How's that for providence?"

I wasn't about to blame God for this one, so I changed the subject. "What did you think of our church?"

She seemed a bit startled by the question but recovered quickly. "You know, I liked it. The music was great and that man who spoke made sense. I'll be back, don't worry. But you won't have to pick me up. I'm picking up Bart. We're going together." She smiled like Sylvester who'd just stuffed Tweety in his mouth and before I could respond, she blew out of the office.

Cherry Cobbler

Thanks to Mrs. Murphy's pep talk, I just whistled to myself and went back to work.

21

I was just getting ready to break for lunch when Grant walked in. "Have you eaten yet?"

"Just getting ready to."

"Would you join me in the garden, Madam?" He bowed low and gestured toward the beautiful, sunny day outside.

I shooed him like a pesky fly, but laughed in spite of myself. Grabbing my sack lunch, which consisted of Mrs. Murphy's leftover chicken, I walked out with him to sit on the bench under the Japanese maple. I smelled the fresh air after the confines of the stuffy office and thanked God that I got to work in a garden.

As I pulled out my chicken, Grant looked at it longingly. I couldn't help but notice that his peanut butter sandwich paled in comparison. "Oh, all right. You can have some. It's way more than I can eat anyway."

I was rewarded with a grin big enough to swallow Manhattan. "Thanks, Cherry. You're the greatest." Without wasting any more words, he dove into that chicken like a starving man. Being single and cooking for himself, perhaps he was. "So, how was your weekend?"

"It was okay," I said cautiously. I didn't want to discuss my love life with Grant.

"That good, huh?"

I decided to change the subject. "What about you? I didn't see you Sunday."

He grinned like he had a secret. "That would be because I wasn't there."

It worked. I bit. "So, where were you?"

"I was on a youth retreat," he announced, as if saying he took a trip on the space shuttle.

"A little old for that, aren't you?"

"Very funny." He refused to let my sarcasm stop his enthusiasm. "I'm volunteering to help with the youth group."

It was my turn to be surprised. "No kidding. What possessed you?"

"I love teenagers, obviously, or I wouldn't be teaching." I waited while he took another bite of that terrific chicken. After chewing, he continued, "But I never had the confidence that I had anything to offer until recently. Somehow winning that award at AA gave me assurance that I really could make a difference." He took another bite and waited for my response.

"That's great, Grant. Those kids are lucky to have you."

"I don't know about that, but they sure challenge me. Do you know that one of those kids worked a summer job and gave half his earnings to a mission organization? And another one started a prayer meeting each day before classes." He shook his head. "I don't think I've ever made such bold stands, but they make me want to."

"What are you talking about? You stood up in front of hundreds of people and told them how Christ helped you overcome alcoholism. That was pretty bold."

He hung his head like a sheepish little boy. "It didn't seem hard. It was actually fun."

"Well, maybe that's the way those kids feel."

"Maybe," he said with doubt in his voice. "Anyway, I love being with them."

"That's great. You have really turned your life around."

"Sometimes I can hardly believe it myself."

"What made you start drinking in the first place?"

"It started in high school. At first it was only on weekends with my friends, but by the end of college I couldn't get through the day without drinking. It numbed me to the hopelessness I felt about life. I don't ever want to go back there again."

Cherry Cobbler

"Any kids like that in youth group?"

"Several. They're the ones I'm drawn to most. Sometimes I hurt for them so much I could cry. I don't want them to go through what I went though."

"How are you going to keep perspective?"

"What do you mean?"

"About the ones that don't make it?"

Grant took off his glasses and rubbed his eyes. "I don't know. I guess I'll cross that bridge when I come to it. But mostly I think it will be realizing that I'm not the one who can decide for someone."

"That's good. You're thinking this through."

"Someone to talk to about those kids, too."

"That seems important."

Grant leaned back and looked up into the leaves of the Maple. We both sat quietly, enjoying the beauty of the day. Suddenly, Grant stood up. "Thanks for the chicken, Cherry. It was great of you to share something that good. I've got to get back." He stood up and whistled as he walked to his car.

After he left, I felt sort of empty, like he was growing in ways I didn't understand. I wondered if I should go back to the soup kitchen. After all, I was good at it and it made me feel useful. This time I could actually concentrate on the people instead of my appearance. The more I thought about it, the better I liked the idea. I decided to call them and start back on Saturday.

22

When I got home from work that night, Crystal called. "How are you doing, Cherry? It's been a million years since I've seen you."

"I'm fine, Crystal. How about you?"

"Good. Sam has been wonderful ever since the event that I will not dignify by mentioning." I imagined her nose sticking up in the air as she said it. "Anyway, why don't you come over for dinner tonight?"

I panicked a little. I never knew what would happen with Crystal in charge, but I'd already opened my refrigerator and realized there was nothing to eat. "All right. Can I bring anything?"

"Nope, just yourself. Seven o'clock okay?"

"Sure."

Dinner with Crystal and Sam was quite the affair. She was an amazing cook and spared no expense on the best ingredients. The centerpiece was always some work of art that she'd concocted. Today it was a clay sculpture she'd designed that looked like three people cheering at a football game. At least that was as close as I could come to figuring it out. I liked it, though. Everything about her dinners was great. For being such a floozy, she sure was a classy entertainer.

When I arrived, she took my coat and pulled me into her living room with a smile as big as the moon. I almost stepped on Twiggy, who looked at me with disdain as she looked at anyone invading her space. Feeling like giving her a small kick, I became immediately distracted as I realized the reason Crystal had invited me over. Sitting on her sofa was the most beautiful man I'd ever seen. At least six feet tall, he had naturally blond hair and blue eyes that burned right through me. His muscular frame swaggered a bit as he stood to his feet to greet me. I tried to keep my eyes off of him but it was an uphill battle. I sat stuffing my face with the elaborate appetizer that Crystal had made, listening to Sam and Tom (that was his name) discuss the latest football game.

I tried not to let my heart get entangled. After all, if Crystal knew this man, he probably didn't have much substance. She most likely met him at the gym and talked him into this dinner.

But he and Sam seemed to hit it off like a house afire and Tom's voice matched his physique.

Cherry Cobbler

After a few minutes Crystal called Sam to the kitchen. Alone with me, Tom initiated conversation. "So, Cherry, Sam tells me you're into drama."

I swallowed the too big piece I had put into my mouth and nodded. "Yes, I write and act in dramas at church."

"I'm in the community playhouse that performs several times a year. I both act and direct."

I began to get interested in spite of myself. "I've always thought that would be fun but never had the time with all my other activities."

"Can you sing?"

I nodded again, wondering where my words had gone.

"Then you should try out for a part in *Seven Brides for Seven Brothers*. I'm going for the lead."

I looked at this incredible man and thought he'd be great in any part. "Maybe I will."

The evening was great. I finally loosened up and Tom laughed at all my jokes. As we were collecting our coats to leave, he leaned over and whispered, "Would you go out with me to the movies this Friday night, Cherry?"

I nodded again suddenly back to the frightened girl I'd been at the beginning of the evening.

"Crystal gave me your number. I'll call and we'll work out the details."

I nodded again, feeling sure I looked like a zombie who'd been placed under a spell.

As soon as I walked into my apartment, the phone rang. I snatched it up; sure it was Tom calling already. To my disappointment, it was Crystal. "Well, what did you think?"

"I've got to admit. He's amazing."

"I knew it! He asked you out, didn't he?"

"Yea, he did."

"I could tell there was some chemistry going on. Now, you've got to play this right, Cherry. Don't blow it!"

I frowned and wished Crystal could see my expression through the phone. "I don't intend to. Besides, it's just one date. It may be all over with after that."

"See, that's what I mean. You can't have that attitude. You've got to hook him right away. Wear something sexy, put on a ton of perfume and invite him in after the evening is over."

"Crystal! I'm not going to do that. You forget I'm a nice church-going girl."

Cherry Cobbler

"Yea and look where it's got you."

"It's got me just fine. I don't need to lose my standards to hook a guy."

"I don't know, Cherry. You should listen to the pro."

I needed to get off the phone fast before I said something I regretted. "Thanks for the dinner, Crystal. It was great. I've got to get some sleep so I can get up for work tomorrow."

"Work, scmurk."

"Bye."

I hung up the phone firmly, feeling mad at Crystal and mad at myself. What kind of guy was Tom anyway? I had no idea. So I did what I'd done countless times before; I called Roslyn.

She agreed to meet me for dinner after work on Tuesday. As soon as we'd ordered, I got right down to it. "I met a guy."

She brightened a little at the thought. Since she was in love, she was a lot more anxious for me to find Mr. Right. "Who is he?"

"His name is Tom. I met him last night, and we have a date this Friday."

"Where'd you meet him?" she asked, still cheerful and expectant. I knew when I answered that question the conversation was going to get interesting.

"At Sam and Crystal's."

Roslyn had just taken a bite of bread, but now she stopped chewing. "He is a Christian, isn't he Cherry?"

"Sure," I blustered. "I'm not going out with a Hindu, for heaven's sake."

"That's not what I mean, and you know it. I mean is he a committed follower of Christ?"

"Well, we haven't actually gotten around to talking about that."

"Cherry! That's the most important thing! How could you not talk about it?"

I looked at my good friend and knew she was talking sense. Suddenly Tom seemed unappealing in spite of his great looks. I couldn't for a minute imagine him helping at the soup kitchen. "You're right, Roslyn. I'll break the date." I soberly took a drink and blinked back tears.

Roslyn reached over and grabbed my hand. "I'm sorry, Cherry. I didn't mean to be so harsh. I know you've wanted this to happen for a long time, and it's getting hard to be patient." She pulled her hand back and added softly, "And I'm sure it's hard to see it happening to me and not to you."

Cherry Cobbler

I looked up in surprise. "No! No, not at all! I love that it's happening to you."

"And you're not just a wee bit jealous?"

"Not really, no. Please don't feel that way around me. I'm thrilled for you and Josh. I'm not jealous."

Roslyn smiled, "You truly are the best friend ever. I'm so lucky to have you."

And with those words I found the courage to refuse Tom kindly when he called me later that night.

23

When Saturday came I eagerly headed for the soup kitchen, looking for what God wanted to do in and through me. After we'd served everyone, I took out the garbage. There, smoking, was a fellow volunteer. Her name was Gloria. She must have been close to forty, although it was hard to tell since she was so weathered by life. She was the kind of woman who always scared me. I'm a rather soft person who cries at commercials with little kids in them and this woman looked as if she'd run out of tears. But she was here, volunteering, which made me think that maybe I'd missed something. I sucked up my courage and spoke, "What do you do for a living, Gloria?"

She puffed deeply on the cigarette, sucking the smoke deep into her lungs. As she coolly blew it out, I felt a bit like running away screaming. Finally she answered, "Wait tables."

I was genuinely surprised, "Wow! You waitress for a living, then come here on Saturdays to volunteer your time? That's really good of you."

Until now she looked as if she were putting up with me the way an older dog would put up with a puppy, but now she gave me her attention. "Not so good. Just a payback."

The woman was not one to waste words. "What do you mean?"

"Spent a bunch of time in places like these. Thankful to be on my own two feet again, so at least I can give something in return." She took another puff and blew a smoke ring.

It was the longest speech I'd heard her give, and I could see it was sincere. I thought of all the people at church who seemed to have their life together but I wondered if they were thankful enough to give something in return. "I admire you, Gloria."

At this she laughed. It was a deep, husky laugh of a woman who's abused her lungs for years. "Can't say anyone ever said that to me before."

I smiled back. "Well, I admire you and hope to get to know you better. Do you have a family?" It was the wrong question; I knew it as soon as it came out of my mouth. Her face fell as if someone had simply erased any emotions. The dead, dull look came back.

"Not anymore."

I decided not to pursue it further, but plunged ahead in another direction. "Would you like to go to the movies with me tonight?"

Our moment of connection was gone. She shook her head. "Nope. Got to work."

"Maybe another time."

She threw her cigarette down and crushed it with her foot, refusing to respond to my suggestion. "Gotta get back in." She walked inside, and I prayed for her fervently.

Toward the end of the time at the kitchen, two of the women we'd served got into a fistfight. It was the punishing, slug-it-out kind of brawl that kids used to get into in grade school. I'd never seen adults go at it like that. As I stood and watched them, wondering what in the world to do, Gloria stepped in, grabbing one of them by the hair. She dragged her off to the side and dropped her like a sack of cloths. Then she went back to the other woman and gave her the same treatment. She didn't say a word, but both women were cowed. No words were needed.

After a short pause in eating, everyone went back to their own business, refusing to acknowledge that anything had disturbed their meal. I started cleaning up, frantically applying all my nervous energy to the serving trays as I scrubbed them. I hoped no one would notice that I was shaking.

Cherry Cobbler

When I got home, I felt depressed. I wished I could fix everyone's problems and I had no clue how to begin. I wanted to reach out to Gloria but she didn't seem to feel that I had anything to offer. Maybe I should try the "church is a great place to meet a man" routine since it worked so well for Mrs. Vanderweide. The idea of Gloria coming to church to meet a man seemed so funny to me that I got the giggles. It's just not in my nature to stay depressed.

I called Roslyn to see if by some miracle she'd be able to go to the movies with me tonight. Of course, she was already taken. I meant it when I told Roslyn that I wasn't jealous of her, but what I didn't tell her was that I was a wee bit jealous of Josh. He was getting all the time I used to have with Roslyn.

I'd resigned myself to an evening alone when Mrs. Vanderweide called. "Hi Cherry," she said, singing my voice like a character in an opera. "Do you want to come over for a party at my place tonight? That new French restaurant in town is catering it and we have a live band. What do you say?"

I was astounded. To be invited to one of Mrs. Vanderweide's parties was unheard of. Only the rich and powerful came to them. "You want me to come?"

"Yes, to thank you for taking me to church."

"Well, okay. What time?"

"Eight o'clock. Got to run. See you there." I thought she'd hung up but she added, "Bring a friend."

As I hung up the phone, I felt a mixture of terror and curiosity. I wasn't sure whether her parties were the kind that good church-going girls went to, but my curiosity won out and I decided to go.

However I didn't want to go alone, so I called Grant. It didn't go so well. "But I don't even know this Mrs. Vanderweide."

"It doesn't matter. She's fabulously wealthy, and you probably won't even get a chance to talk to her. It's just a night of good food and rich people."

"I don't know, Cherry. I don't think I'd fit in."

"Me either, Grant! That's why I need company."

"Well, when you put it like that…"

"Then you'll go?"

"I guess so."

"Good, I'll pick you up about eight thirty. Wear that new suit."

"Oh gee." His voice had the tone of man who was about to face surgery.

I smiled to myself as I hung up the phone. It really was kind of a nasty thing to do to Grant. I picked out a silk pantsuit that made me look like an overgrown butterfly, but it was the only thing I had that seemed appropriate. After picking up Grant, who once again looked fabulous, I parked my cheap little compact next to BMWs and Mercedes. As I walked up to her mansion, I thought about what an amazing day this had been. How could I experience such extremes all in one day?

Once inside, I marveled at the carpet which was so thick that it felt like walking on a mattress. The hallway was as big as my whole apartment and five times taller. The chandelier that hung from the ceiling was approximately the same size as my bathroom. Grant stared at everything like he was at the zoo. "Who is this lady?" he asked.

"She has a makeup line."

"Whoa. I had no idea makeup was so lucrative."

It took me a while to find Mrs. Vanderweide, even though she was dressed gaudy enough to attract a swarm of bees. When I did, she only gave me a few words of gushing welcome, which was all I heard from her all evening. She noticed Grant though, and turned on all her charm. It didn't get her anywhere since he was as taciturn as a telephone post.

As we walked away, I couldn't help teasing him. "Wasn't she your type?"

"Very funny. Let's find the food."

Since we didn't know anyone, we spent most of the evening eating and gawking at the furnishings and powerful people in attendance. I recognized the mayor, the president of my bank, and the editor of the newspaper. Grant saw the Channel Five news team.

A few people talked to me but as soon as they found out I was nobody, they hurried on for another contact. More than a few women noticed Grant but once they realized he was a history teacher, he was history. We were just about to give it up and go home when I heard a commotion outside. We stepped out to the pool area, which was beautifully landscaped by the way, and saw two men in an all-out brawl. Unfortunately, Gloria wasn't here to break it up. I shook my head and walked back through the house to go home. Human nature seemed the same no matter what the trimmings.

We spent a long time sitting in my car talking after I drove him home. "Do you think you'd like to be that rich, Cherry?"

"No. Too much of a burden. And I'd feel like I was living in somebody's museum. I'm more the little bungalow with a white picket fence kind of girl."

He smiled. "That's what I thought."

"What about you?"

Cherry Cobbler

"No way. I'm the cabin in the woods sort of guy. You know, twig furniture, bear skin rugs, that sort of thing."

"Yuck! You want dead animals on your floors?"

He looked annoyed. "Maybe just a couple."

"Well, to each his own." We sat in silence for a minute, each lost in thoughts of a future that didn't include our apartments. "Do you think you'll ever get tired of teaching?"

"Nope. I love it. I could see getting a graduate degree though and teaching college level."

"I could see that. Professor Grant. It fits."

"What about you? Always an office administrator?"

"No! I kind of fell into that. It was never a career goal."

"So what would you like to do?"

I sighed. "I don't want to tell you."

"Oh come on, try me. I won't tell a soul."

"You promise?"

"Scout's honor."

I looked at him suspiciously. "Were you ever a scout?"

"Uh, no. How about, cross my heart, hope to die, stick a needle in my eye."

"That's disgusting! I hate that saying. No, I won't let you promise that way." I crossed my arms in front of me and gave my most authoritative look.

"Well then, how about what Jesus says: 'Let your yes be yes and your no be no.' I say I'll keep my promise, so you'll just have to believe me."

"Oh for heaven's sake, if you're going to quote Scripture, I guess I'll have to trust you." I looked out the window even though it was pitch black and I couldn't see anything.

"So what do you want to be?"

I forced it out. "A mom."

"Oh." He was so quiet that my embarrassment grew. He probably thought I'd been reincarnated out of the dark ages. But then he added, "That's great. I never hear women admit that anymore."

"You're just saying that."

He turned to look me in the eye. "I don't just say things, Cherry. If I say it, I mean it." His voice had enough of an edge to it that I knew he was serious.

"So you don't think that's a dumb goal?"

"I think it's a wonderful goal. It's from the same root as my love of teaching. It's wanting to mold and shape a human life – to make a difference for eternity. How could that be dumb?"

I wanted to hug him. I hadn't said out loud that I wanted to be a mom to anyone. Not to Roslyn, not to Jeannie, not even to Mrs. Murphy. It felt good to voice that longing. "Thanks, Grant." Then I was done being serious. "But since that seems unlikely to happen, I guess I'd better figure out something practical, like developing a makeup line or a new way to lose 500 pounds."

Grant refused to join my jest. "Why is it unlikely?"

"Well, babies come out of marriage. At least that's what I was always taught, and I don't want to try for one any other way."

"So you've given up on marriage for good then?"

"Of course not, but it seems a bit elusive at the moment." I made a face to emphasize the point.

He laughed. "It can creep up on you all of sudden. Watch out!"

"You sound like you have experience in this field," I said with a lilt in my voice.

"Maybe a little."

I was just about to pry when he said, "Well, church tomorrow; got to get some sleep. Thanks for inviting me. I think." And he walked off into the moonlight.

24

When I walked into church on Sunday morning, Mrs. Vanderweide greeted me with a stunning smile as she clung to Mr. Finster's arm. She was once again dressed conservatively and I wondered if he had any idea what she was like. Either way, I was glad she was at church and sitting with someone other than me. I know. Great attitude on my part, but that's the way I felt.

Grant sidled up to me a few minutes later. "She looks a bit different than she did last night, huh?"

"Just a bit."

"What's with this guy?"

"I have no idea." I shook my head as if I were trying to figure out the square root of something.

"Well, it takes all kinds. It sure can't hurt for Mrs. Vanderweide to be at church."

"Maybe."

"Maybe?"

"Yea, who knows? Pretty soon she may have every woman here wearing bizarre colors of lipstick, and the

Cherry Cobbler

men dyeing their hair." When Grant raised his eyebrows, I nodded, "That's right. She's expanding to a men's line now."

"Oh great, thanks for the warning. I'll steer clear from now on."

"As if you wouldn't have before."

When I got home from church, I used what little discipline I had and ate a Healthy Choice meal instead of ice cream. As I swallowed the low fat food I looked longingly at the telephone, wishing Mrs. Murphy would call with an offer of a meal.

I'd settled down to a good book, spent a relaxing afternoon, and was just thinking about dinner when I heard a great deal of honking outside my apartment building. Since my apartment had an excellent view of the parking lot (not a selling point), I looked out and saw a black convertible. The person in the car looked way too much like Crystal. Sure enough, as soon as she spotted me she waved wildly and started honking again.

If I hadn't looked, I might have been able to pretend I wasn't home, but there was no going back now. I pulled on a jacket and walked out to her, feeling as though I was going to a funeral – my own.

"Come on. Hurry. Come see my new toy!" Crystal continued to wave and honk as she bounced in the seat. Others were looking out their windows now, and I wondered if the apartment complex would vote to kick me out.

"Where'd this come from?" was all I managed to squeak out.

"Sam bought it for me."

"I guess Sam is doing okay at work."

"Yes, now that he's applying himself to work instead of the women at the office, he got a raise. Get in. Let's go for a ride."

I looked at the car and then back at my apartment, trying madly to think of some excuse. Crystal seemed to figure out what I was doing and counteracted it. When she made up her mind, it didn't matter what anyone else thought. "Oh come on. We both know you don't have anything else to do. Get in."

I sighed and slipped in. Now Crystal is not a good driver at any time, but in a flashy new sports car she makes the Daytona 500 look like a Sunday afternoon drive. Before I could even fasten my seatbelt, she roared out of the parking lot, laying rubber all the way. I figured poor Sam would have to replace the tires after the first five thousand miles.

Cherry Cobbler

She headed out to the country, which gave me a little peace. We were less likely to hit any pedestrians there. I feared for the raccoon population though. If we hit a deer, it would probably just sail over the hood and land in the back seat. Crystal would most likely demand that Sam skin it and make a coat for her out of it.

As her speedometer approached 100, she suddenly slammed on her brakes so that she wouldn't hit the truck in front of us. If I hadn't been buckled up, I would have ended up in the bed of the truck.

Glancing around it, she passed on a double yellow line and zoomed into place just as a car coming from the other direction reached us. The entire time she chatted away about a new outfit she'd just bought, not noticing that my knuckles were white from hanging on to the dash.

After a few more close calls, she turned around and took me back home. Angels must have been watching over the animal population that night since we had no new pelts in the back seat. That, or we were going so fast that I didn't notice. Anyway, when she pulled in I sat there for a moment, trying to decide if it was safe to unbuckle.

"So, what do you think of Bessie?"

"Who?"

"That's what I named my car."

"You named your car a cow name?"

"You think Bessie is a cow name?" She frowned and stuck her lip out so far, you could have hung a coat on it. "Now you've ruined it for me. What'd ya have to go and do that for?"

"Sorry."

"Oh, that's okay. Are you ready for my really big news?"

"Bigger than Bessie?"

"Way bigger."

"I guess so." I didn't feel like getting out yet anyway. My stomach was a little woozy.

She wiggled down in her seat and clapped her hands together like a little kid. "You are going to be an aunt!"

I looked at her a minute in horror. All I could think of was a tiny baby who wore leopard skins and squealed in terror as her mother roared around in a convertible. It was not a pretty picture. "You're having a baby?"

"Yep! And I'm not naming it Bessie, although I do like the name a lot." She paused to look in the rearview mirror to reapply her lipstick. "So what do you think of our news?"

"Wow, what can I say? A baby."

She looked away from the mirror and stared at me. "You don't seem very excited."

Cherry Cobbler

"Oh, I'm overwhelmed."

"Good. Cause we'll count on you a lot to help out. I don't know nothin' about babies."

"I'm not exactly an expert myself."

"I know, but you're the motherly type. It will just come natural to you." Suddenly she became serious. "I'm really scared, Cherry. What if I'm a terrible mother?"

I couldn't tell her what I really thought, that as far as I could tell she would be a terrible mother, so instead I lied. "You'll be fine. It will just take some getting used to."

"That's what Sam says. It's just that it's not like taking a job. You can't just quit if it's not working out."

"True."

"Will you help me?"

"I'll try."

"Good, that's what I wanted to know. Well, thanks for helping me break in Bessie. Call if you ever want to take a spin in her."

I just smiled and walked gingerly back into my apartment. I lost my appetite for dinner. I still wasn't sure whether I'd be able to keep lunch down. Part of it was from the car ride, but I was also pretty bummed about the baby.

How could God let her be a mother and not me?
Sometimes nothing makes sense.

Roslyn called me at work on Monday. "Can we meet for dinner tonight?"

"What…is Josh out of town or something?"

"No, I just want to eat with you."

"Wow, do I ever rate! I beat out Josh."

"Yea, well, you know how it is."

"Yea, well, no I don't"

"Are you all right, Cherry?"

I sighed and pulled myself together. "I'm fine. Sorry for being such a smart aleck."

"That's all right. I expect that."

"Oh, stop it!"

"Okay." I could hear her grinning over the phone. "I'll pick you up about six-thirty."

"It's a date."

Cherry Cobbler

The day couldn't go fast enough. I was still mad at God for allowing Crystal to be a mom. What could He be thinking? I planned on asking Roslyn what she thought.

When she picked me up, she was humming, which was very un-Roslyn like. "What's with you?"

"Oh nothing," she said mysteriously, implying that there was definitely something.

As we settled down at the restaurant, I was tired of waiting. "Out with it, lady. What's up?"

"Should we order first?"

"Nope. Out with it now."

"Okay, are you ready for this?"

"Well, I can't know that until you tell me, can I?"

"All right. Josh and I are engaged."

I should have been prepared. I should have known it was coming any minute, but for some reason I'd refused to read the signs. When the words were out of Roslyn's mouth, they felt like bullets and I did the one thing I didn't want to do. I cried.

Somehow I managed to convince her that they were tears of joy. I guess that's what she really wanted to believe, and to some extent they were. The trouble was that before Crystal's announcement, I was already feeling cheated. Now I felt like the loneliest woman on earth.

I got through the meal by falling back on my jolly old persona, cracking every joke I could think of, keeping the tears at bay. But as soon as I was back in my apartment, all my reserve crumbled and I cried buckets. I had just reached the hiccupping stage when the phone rang. Like an idiot I picked it up.

"Hello," I said as I gulped for air.

"Cherry, is that you?"

"Yea, it's me."

"What's wrong?"

"I can't talk about it right now, Grant. Why are you calling, anyway?"

"I'm calling everyone in Bible study to see if we can get a potluck going this Sunday, but I'm glad to talk if you need someone."

With that, I blurted. "Crystal is pregnant."

There was silence. "Who's Crystal?"

"My sister-in-law."

"Oh yea, the leopard skin one. I met her once when she was staying with you."

Cherry Cobbler

"Real motherly type, huh?"

"Not exactly the way I'd describe her. Is that what's got you so upset?"

"Yea, that and Roslyn's engagement. It's all too much for one weekend."

"I see. Crystal's having the baby you want, and Roslyn's having the marriage you want."

How does he do that? "Stupid, isn't it?"

"No, Cherry. It's not stupid. Are you mad at God?"

"A little." I paused and felt guilty. "Okay, a lot. I don't know how to get over being mad at Him."

"Read Job 38."

"That's going to help?"

"I can almost guarantee it."

After Grant hung up, I opened my Bible and read the words of the Lord: "Where were you when I laid the earth's foundation? Tell me, if you understand." I didn't stop reading until I got to chapter forty-two where Job says, "Surely I spoke of things I did not understand, things too wonderful for me to know."

I closed my Bible, confessed my ignorance and slept peacefully.

25

In the morning, I could see things more clearly. I even began to look forward to going shopping with Roslyn for a wedding dress and being her maid of honor. Except I dreaded hearing my mother say "always a bridesmaid, never a bride" one more time. It had ceased being funny about five years ago, but she still liked saying it.

For some inexplicable reason that I cannot possibly explain, that made me want to call her. As soon as she heard my voice, she said, "Can you believe it? I finally get to be a grandma!"

I was so glad I was in a better place than yesterday. "I know, and I get to be an aunt and Dad gets to be a grandpa and Sam gets to be a dad."

"Boy, you're a sharp one. Figure that out all by yourself did you?"

"Yep. You didn't raise no dummies."

"Hmmm."

"Guess what else?"

"You're getting married!"

"Close. Roslyn is. She's asked me to be her maid of honor."

"Ah, always a bridesmaid, never a bride." There is something wonderful about always knowing what someone is going to say.

"That's me."

"You sound pretty cheerful about it."

"I am. It couldn't happen to a nicer person."

"That's for sure. I like that Roslyn."

"Me, too."

"You're not blue about the fact that it's not you?"

"I was, but I got over it."

"You sure you don't want me to set you up with Edgar Martin?"

"Absolutely sure."

"Your loss."

"My loss."

"You're sure in an agreeable mood. How about if we plan a baby shower for Crystal?"

"That would be fun." And I meant it, but I had to add, "Do you think Crystal will be able to handle motherhood?"

Cherry Cobbler

"I have to admit that it's hard to picture. But it's amazing the things that change when a baby comes on the scene. Did you know that I used to have a Harley before Sam was born?"

"What!"

"Yep."

"Why haven't I ever see pictures of you on it?"

"I guess I never thought of having my picture taken; just liked riding it."

"So, why haven't you gotten another one since we're all grown up?"

"Actually, I'm thinking about it."

"This I'd have to see. Did Dad ride?"

"Noo. He was scared to death of it. I think he gave a thank offering at church the day I sold it."

"So what would he think of it now?"

"He's gotten braver as he's gotten older. He's talking about getting matching ones."

"This is going to take some getting used to – my parents, the riders. Just don't join any gangs. You do have a grandchild coming that you have to be an example for."

"We'll try to avoid them for the child's sake," she said with sarcasm dripping like rain.

"This conversation has been enlightening. I'm going to go now so I can get to work and spend the rest of the day pondering these revelations."

"Okay, honey. By the way, you haven't visited for a while."

"You either."

"True." There was a pause while we both felt guilty. "I love you, Cherry blossom."

"You haven't called me that in years. This grandkid stuff must be getting to you."

"I hope so."

"I love you, too, Mom."

I'd just settled down at work when a woman I'd never seen before walked in. She was dressed in a nicely tailored blue suit, had short brown hair and was carrying a briefcase. When I asked if I could help her, I got a shock.

"Are you Cherry?"

Surprised, I answered before I thought better of it. "Yes, I am."

Cherry Cobbler

"Sam is your brother?"

My throat started to tighten and I began to sweat. "Yes," I said hesitantly.

She sat down and to my dismay, began to cry. "Will you help me?" she gasped between sobs.

"With what?" I really couldn't imagine.

"To get your brother back."

"What?"

"I can't stand it. I see him every day at the office, and he acts like I don't even exist. I want him back." She stopped crying long enough to blow her nose loudly. I looked at her in amazement. What did these women see in my brother? They were more desperate than I was.

"Why come to me?"

She sniffed and pulled herself together. "Well, I needed some gardening help and Sam told me you worked here. I didn't know where else to turn."

Lord, help me. "Well, I'm sure I can't do anything."

"Oh, but you can. Your brother thinks a lot of you. He'd listen."

It was time to put a stop to this. "Kim…your name is Kim isn't it?"

She nodded.

"You need to know that Sam really loves Crystal. He regrets ever cheating on her."

"But I know he saw something in me. We clicked like ham and rye. If he'd just give me a chance…"

"Take my advice and move on."

"Why?" she cried as if I'd told her to jump off a cliff.

"Because Sam and Crystal are going to have a baby."

At this her eyes opened wide. I was ready for another crying jag, but instead she pulled out her tissues, wiped her eyes and straightened her shoulders. Her voice took on a clipped, business tone. "Well, why didn't you say so in the first place? I don't mind taking a man away from his wife, but a child's another thing. I do have my standards." And she picked up her briefcase, turned around, and walked out the door.

When I got home from work that night I was tired. I didn't want to talk to anybody or see anybody. I wanted to soak in a hot bath and read a book. I'd managed to do just that when the phone rang. I let voicemail pick up and continued to soak.

After an extra long bath, I sank down onto the sofa and luxuriated in having no responsibilities for the moment, when my doorbell began to ring repeatedly. I tried to ignore it, but when it rang continuously for at least ten times, I finally gave up and answered it. To my joy, it was Crystal.

She burst into the room in her normal reserved style. "Why didn't you answer the phone?"

"I was in the bathtub."

"You should have gotten out. It was important."

"Evidently," I said as dryly as I could. It was lost on Crystal.

"Have you seen Twiggy?"

My brain went to mush for a minute, with no idea how to answer.

"My cat, Twiggy. Has she been here?"

"Uh, no," I said, hoping that would end it and she would leave.

"Well, where is she?"

What, did she think I'd kidnapped her? "I'm sure I don't know."

"But this is the only other home she knows. She has to be here." And she began looking under the sofa and then headed for the bedroom. I grabbed her just as she started throwing things out of my closet.

"Crystal, she's not here." I emphasized each word as if she was hard of hearing, hoping volume and emphasis would win the day. She ignored me and continued to ransack my closet.

After most everything was on the floor of my room, she walked back into the living room and sank down on the sofa. "I guess she's not here."

I thought about putting one of my sofa pillows over her face and holding it, but instead I said, "That's what I said. Don't you think I'd notice a cat in my apartment? After all, it's not that big."

"But Twiggy is sensitive and shy. She's a real lady. She doesn't always make her presence known."

This was an interesting definition of a lady coming from Crystal. "Well, I promise to call if she shows up." I lifted her arm up to help her off the sofa and pulled her toward the door. It didn't work.

She stopped at the chair nearest the door. "What will I do if I can't find her?" The look on her face almost made me feel sorry for her, but then I glanced back at the bedroom.

"She'll be back. After all, she loves you as much as you love her."

Crystal looked at me and her eyes flooded with tears, "She's the only one who has ever really loved me."

"That's not true. Sam adores you."

Cherry Cobbler

She waved that away as trivial. "Well, of course, Sam. He can't help himself. But Twiggy loves me for who I am, not how I look or what I do for her."

Okay, that did it. I had to be more forceful. "Why don't you go on home? She's probably there waiting for you right now."

This thought seemed to sink in. "All right, but call me if she comes here."

"I will."

"You promise?"

"I promise."

I sighed with relief when she'd gone and quickly locked the door. When the phone rang fifteen minutes later, I let the machine pick it up, but I heard Crystal wail, "She's not here!" Instead, I dialed Roslyn's number.

"Hi, Cherry, what's up?"

"Can a person divorce her sister-in-law?"

26

"Cherry, can you come over tonight and practice this drama for Sunday?" Jeannie's sweet voice came over the line and I jumped at the chance to spend an evening with somebody normal.

"Sure. What time?"

"Is seven too early?"

"Not at all. See you then."

I hung up the phone and gave my attention to my boss as he explained where he'd be for the next few hours. "Now if Mrs. Vanderweide comes in, tell her I'll be out all afternoon."

"Yes sir!"

"Have you heard the latest thing she wants to do?"

I shook my head, not sure I wanted to hear the answer. "She wants to pay for the homeless shelter to be landscaped. What do you think of that?"

"I'm amazed and shocked. This is quite out of character, but really nice," I added, feeling I was being disloyal.

Cherry Cobbler

"Extremely nice. I'm wondering what has wrought such a change."

"Maybe she's got religion."

Mr. Hopkins laughed out loud. "That'll be the day. See you later, Cherry. Hold down the fort."

After he left, I thought about Mrs. Vanderweide. The Pastor had talked about ministering to the poor on Sunday. Maybe she really was listening. Time would tell.

That evening when I arrived at Jeannie's she was fresh from working out. She looked like a pro in her velour sweat pants. I wondered what I'd look like in a pair of those. I imagined I'd look like a blue Popsicle. Oh well, I liked Popsicles.

"Cherry, I love this drama you wrote. You've missed your calling."

"I seemed to have missed a lot of things."

Jeannie put her hands on her thirty-four inch hips and scolded, "Why do you always do that?"

"Do what?"

"Run yourself down."

I smiled. "That way I always beat everyone else to it."

"No one feels that way about you. Everybody loves you."

"Thanks, Jeannie."

"I mean it."

"I know you do. That's what I like about you. I feel that you accept me even if I do overeat and never exercise."

"Would you like help?"

"With what?"

"The eating and exercise thing."

"No!"

"Okay."

"I'm sorry. It's just that I've been on a million diets and a thousand exercise programs. Now I'm working on accepting myself just the way I am."

"That's great. Everyone else accepts you, so you should accept yourself."

"My opinion exactly."

"I'll never bring it up again, except to tell you I like you just the way you are."

"Thanks. So what did you like about my drama?"

"Well, for one, it had me in stitches. But just when you had me roaring with laughter, you slapped me with some amazing truth that burned into my soul. It's better than the ones we order."

"Wow, that's quite a compliment. I guess I'll have to write some more."

"Please do. Now, if you could help me figure out who would be right for the other parts...?"

We spent about an hour working on the drama then we had a cup of coffee and visited. "So Cherry, what's new at the garden center?"

"Well, we have a new rose bush that's pretty amazing."

"That's not what I meant. I mean with your job."

"Nothing new. Just the same ol', same ol'."

"Who was sitting with you at church a couple of weeks ago?"

"Mrs. Vanderweide, the richest woman in town, and the craziest."

"That's great that she came to church."

I narrowed my gaze. "She came to meet men."

Jeannie's eyebrows shot up. "Who gave her that idea?"

I looked at the ceiling and feigned ignorance.

"Ah, interesting form of evangelism."

I shrugged my shoulders. "Whatever works."

"Well, what about your love life? Any news there?"

"I wish!"

"What about Grant?"

"What about him?"

"You two seem to get along really well."

"Yea, we're good friends. I can talk to him about anything. He's like a brother that I actually like."

"Nothing more?"

"With Grant? No."

"Okay. I just wondered."

"Roslyn and Josh are engaged, though."

"I heard that."

"What do you think?"

"I think it's great."

We finally exhausted all the topics we could think of. I said my goodbyes and headed home, thankful that I'd been with a nice, calm, normal person.

Cherry Cobbler

As soon as I got home I put on my pajamas and turned on the TV, ready for an hour of mindless dribble. But something was wrong with my box. There was some unearthly sound coming from it. Then I decided it wasn't coming from the TV, but that some woman or child in the apartment complex was screaming. I muted the sound and listened. Whoever it was sounded as if she were right outside my door. I looked through the peephole, but couldn't see anyone. So I nervously opened the door. In shot a tan and brown furry stick.

27

I couldn't believe it. Twiggy had actually gotten through the security system and into my hallway. I tried to pick her up, but she yowled like a banshee and swiped me with her declawed paw, running under my bed just beyond reach.

I sighed and picked up the phone. "Crystal?"

"Yea?"

"Someone is here to see you."

"Twiggy?" She screamed so loud that I had to hold the phone away from my ear. "I'll be right over!"

So much for my one night with a normal person.

Crystal swung in with all the grace of Tarzan (dressed similar to him, too). She wiggled her tightly clad derriere under my bed and pulled Twiggy out, the cat yowling as if her tail was being cut off. When I saw that Crystal actually had Twiggy by the tail, I thought she had some reason for protest. As Twiggy tried wildly to get away, Crystal cradled her closely, crooning to her in the drivel in which we talk to our pets, soothing the wild beast within that emaciated body. After a while she began to calm down and soon she was purring. It was my first glimpse at the hope that Crystal may actually be able to handle motherhood.

She sat down and continued to pet Twiggy into a sort of stupor, singing her lullabies almost on key. After a while she whispered to me, "Open the door to her cage, and I'll pop her in. She'll make it home now."

I did as I was told and stepped back for a repeat performance of the angry howling. But instead, Twiggy seemed to understand she was going home and curled back down to sleep. Crystal hugged me and still whispering said, "Thank you for taking care of her until I got here. I don't know what I'd do without her."

You know, I believed her.

With Twiggy home safe and sound, I was sure the rest of the week would be calm. But within a day, I got a call from Gloria.

"Cherry?"

"Yes?"

"Can you come bail me out of jail?"

"You're in jail?"

"No, I'm at Disney World. Can you come?"

"Sure."

I got in my car and wondered what to expect. I'd never bailed anyone out of jail before. I wondered if I could afford it. And what did she do, rob a bank? Kill someone?

I pulled up to the station and went in, looking like a fish out of water. "I'm here for Gloria," I said to the nearest official looking person, who turned out to be a taxi driver. He pointed me to an officer.

"You have the fifty dollars to spring her?"

"I think so." Fortunately I had grocery money in my purse. I took it out and reluctantly watched the officer tuck it away.

"We'll bring her out."

"Officer?"

"Yea?"

"What's she in for?"

"Her boyfriend charged her with battery."

"Her boyfriend?"

"Yea, he's a little guy," he said in explanation.

Gloria came out looking like a bull that has just had a red flag waved in front of his nose. I questioned the battery charge until I saw her and then wondered how badly the poor guy got beat up.

"I'll pay ya back."

"That's okay."

She puffed herself up like a cobra. "I don't like to be in debt to nobody."

I nodded. She was not one to argue with.

When we were outside, she started walking away. "My car's right here, Gloria."

"I'll take the bus."

"I don't mind."

"I'll take the bus!"

And there was no more to say about it. She was soon out of sight.

When I saw Gloria on Saturday at the soup kitchen, she walked up to me without a word and handed me a fifty-dollar bill. I stared at it for a minute, wondering what to say. As it turned out we never said a word to one another. She acted like I didn't exist. I decided to let it go, mostly because I was scared to death of her.

That night I went out with Grant, Josh, and Roslyn for dinner and a movie. It was such a relief. None of them demanded anything of me and they were all as comfortable as old shoes. When I told them all about my week's adventures, they stared openmouthed.

"I don't think I ever had to deal with anything that crazy in Romania," Roslyn said. "By the way, Josh and I are going back there after we get married."

"You are?" Grant and I both said at once. He and I looked at each other, reading the sadness with both felt. We both would be losing our best friends.

Josh noticed and was quick to add, "Not for at least six months, but Roslyn has told me all about what she did there and it's amazing. We'll make a great medical team."

"Yes, you will," I said with true affection.

"You'll both come to visit, won't you?" Roslyn asked, looking like a curly haired doll, much too young to be married or a doctor.

"Sure we will," said Grant, trying to sound cheerful. None of us believed that his voice reflected his feelings.

After that, the gathering was just a little more sober. I looked at them and realized I'd come to depend on our foursome. I wasn't sure what I'd do without it.

Cherry Cobbler

Grant brought up the subject on the way home. "You know our social life is going to go to pieces when those two leave."

"As if it had much oomph anyway."

"True, but at least it's better than sitting home watching TV."

"Most true."

We were silent for a minute then Grant spoke again. "I've wanted to ask you something, Cherry." The way his tone of voice changed worried me. I wasn't sure what was coming.

"Yes?" I asked, wishing I wouldn't have to.

"You know that I'm volunteering with the youth group?"

I nodded.

"Well, we need more sponsors for a retreat next weekend. I think you'd be great. Why don't you come?"

I looked at him as if he'd asked me to clean toilets all weekend. "Are you kidding?"

"No. Cherry, you'd be great with those young girls. They would love you."

"I don't know." I couldn't believe I was even considering it. It must have been the thought of being loved by a teenager. Certainly a novel idea.

"Come on. It's at a beautiful retreat center with really nice cabins, and you wouldn't have to cook all weekend. Everyone tells me this place has great food."

The rat, he knew that would seal the deal. "Well, I guess I could try it once."

"That's great, Cherry. You will love it."

I got home and wondered what I could be thinking. Oh well, I had until the weekend; surely I'd think of some excuse by then not to go.

28

The rest of the week went by and I couldn't think of one single excuse. I got to Friday and felt panicked. What could I possibly offer a bunch of teenage girls? They'd probably hate me and make fun of me after they put my bra in the freezer and short-sheeted my bed. I packed with a certain dread that I'd regret this weekend for the rest of my life.

By the time I arrived at the church with my bag, I'd amassed a great deal of anger toward Grant. When he cheerfully said hi, I gave him a look that could slice him in two. He seemed startled, but I showed no mercy. "I'm going to poison you or push you off a cliff this weekend, Grant. You will be so sorry you got me into this."

"Hey, I just asked. I didn't force you at knifepoint."

"It doesn't matter. You're responsible and I'm gunning for you."

The one thing that was good was that we didn't have a church bus. I had three girls in my car, and I got to drive. I liked that better. If worse came to worse, I'd jump in my car and come home.

Fortunately the girls in my car were the nice, polite kind. They must have shown mercy on me because I was the new recruit. I didn't have to endure any camp songs or crude jokes. They simply asked questions about me, and I did the same with them. The time together flew by.

The camp was only about an hour away and I had to admit that it was beautiful. A wooded setting complete with a lake and individual cabins, it looked like the kind of getaway most people in the city tried to find. I had seven girls in my room that I was responsible for, the three who'd been in my car and four more. A couple of the girls looked as though they could carve me up and eat me for supper, but my experience at the soup kitchen had taken some of my fear of tough women away. I could handle them.

We started the evening with some vigorous singing led by a youth worship band. Other than needing a hearing aid at the end of the evening, I really enjoyed it. The kids jumped up and down and showed more enthusiasm than a child at Disneyland. I thought we ought to let them lead worship at home sometime. They'd wake us all up.

After worship, we had to do bag skits. Each group of eight was given a paper bag full of small props. We had to look at the props and come up with a skit using each of them. This was my kind of thing. I was the drama queen.

There were a few other kids who loved the activity, getting into it right away. The more retiring types were glad to let us go to it, just asking what we wanted them to do. We ended up creating our own mini version of *The Lord of the Rings*. I got to be the dwarf since, as one kid put it, I was vertically challenged. It was great success and we were given the evening's Oscar. This seemed to seal my popularity with the group. I was almost signing autographs by the end of the evening.

"So, have you forgiven me yet?" Grant asked with a smile as he walked by me when I was surrounded by a group of adoring fans.

I didn't want to give in so easily, so I gave a sly look. "Maybe…the weekend's not over yet."

"It just gets better."

"We'll see."

About two in the morning I was ready to ring his neck. Each time I almost fell asleep, someone would start talking and laughing again. Finally I sat up, announced that the next person who spoke was sleeping outside, and put my head back down with it quiet enough to hear a pin drop.

I wasn't quite so popular the next day. A few of the girls looked at me as if I was the Wicked Witch of the West. Clearly they'd decided that when cabin sponsors had been handed out that they got gypped. One girl told me that she was grateful that I'd said something. She'd wanted to sleep.

We had a speaker in the morning, which the night owls from the night before had a great deal of trouble paying attention to, and in the afternoon we broke for sports. Knowing that I'd always hated sports at youth retreats, I offered to teach a drama class. I got a handful of kids to come with me, and we tried out all sorts of skit ideas. I recruited a few of them for our dramas at church.

Best of all, however, was a conversation I had with one girl at the end of the day. I'd noticed that she spent a lot of time alone and that she looked at the other kids with longing, like a child looking in the window of a toy store when she had no money. She was overweight, not particularly attractive and obviously shy.

My opportunity to talk to her came when the other kids took off to play Capture the Flag. This girl stayed back, and I sat down next to her. "Hi, my name is Cherry."

She snorted at my introduction. "Your parents named you Cherry?"

"Yea, they never really liked me."

"I guess not."

"What's your name?"

"Jacqueline."

Cherry Cobbler

"A much more dignified name than Cherry." She just shrugged her shoulders. "So is this your first retreat?"

"Naw, I've been to lots."

"What's your favorite part?"

She seemed to give this some thought. "Being away from my parents."

That wasn't what I'd expected. That was a negative reason, not a positive one. I decided to ignore it. "What year in school are you?"

"Senior."

"Any plans for next year?"

"College."

"Do you know which one?"

She shook her head. I was thinking that perhaps the conversation was over when she said, "Do you believe all this God stuff?"

"Every word."

"Why?"

Her question made me stop and think. I don't think anyone had ever asked me that before. I wanted to get it right. "Because I see evidence of Him all around, especially in my own life. Without God I'd be pretty unbearable. He's helped me see my flaws and given me ways to deal with them. Not that I don't have a long way to go, but I can see how far I've come."

She looked ahead, not at me. "I can't stand to look at my flaws."

"You don't have any more than the rest of us, you know."

Now I had her attention. "Look at me," she said as if that explained everything.

"Are you talking about your physical appearance?"

"Of course I am." She looked away in disgust. "You wouldn't understand."

"Why not?"

"Because you're beautiful."

I could not have been more shocked if I'd been struck by lightning. "But I'm overweight."

She snorted again as she had at the beginning. "That doesn't matter because you're proportioned right and your face is lovely. I don't have any of that."

Which goes to show that everything is in your own perception of yourself. "If there's one thing I've learned, Jacqueline, it's that God made me just the way He wants me and that my life would be all wrong if I looked like some supermodel or something. I wouldn't be the person

He created me to be. Most of life is learning to be content with what God gives us in every respect."

"Now you sound like my grandma." She said it rolling her eyes, but she actually smiled a bit.

"Then she's a wise woman."

"Like you?" she grinned.

I nodded and knew we were going to be okay from now on.

That night, everyone went to sleep a lot earlier out of exhaustion and the next morning I felt downright civil toward Grant. He sat down next to me at breakfast. "So, what do you think?"

"I think you're off the hook."

"I noticed that you and Jacqueline connected."

"Yea."

"Nobody's gotten more than three words out of her all year. You're a miracle worker."

"Well, we have a lot in common."

"What are you talking about? You're the most talkative person I know. I'll bet you were in the middle of everything that was happening in high school."

"That's true, but I felt like Jacqueline does inside. I just knew how to cover it up with lots of bravado."

"Well, at any rate, it was worth you coming along, just for her if for no other reason."

I nodded.

"So you're not going to kill me anymore? No sudden death made to look like an accident?"

"I still might. Not this weekend though."

He smiled. He had a great smile.

29

I came back glad that I'd gone and determined to look for Jacqueline at church from now on. I decided to call her Tuesday night. We got together for a coke and talked. It was nice and made me feel useful.

Mrs. Vanderweide came into work the following day, and it wasn't even Monday. "What are you doing here?" I asked a little too abruptly.

She didn't notice. "What time do you get off work?"

"Five," I said suspiciously.

"Okay, go straight home."

"Why?" I was starting to get a sharp pain in my neck.

"Because an interior designer will be there at five-thirty."

"Whatever for?"

She smiled. "To redesign your apartment, of course, silly."

I looked at her in horror. "My apartment is fine."

"Oh honey, you can't be serious. I know you can't afford much on your salary."

I was wishing at the moment that Gloria was here so she could take a swing at her for me. "Really, Mrs. Vanderweide, I'm perfectly content with my apartment."

"Well, he'll be there at five-thirty. Don't keep him waiting. Rolf doesn't like to be kept waiting." And she left as I tried to figure out how to protest.

I fumed for the rest of the day, wondering what I was going to do with Rolf. There seemed no recourse but to face him firmly and send him away as soon as he arrived.

I found out that Rolf was punctual. No sooner had I hung up my coat and put my slippers on than I heard one loud rap on my door. It was exactly five twenty-nine according to my watch.

Rolf wore a black turtleneck that fit as tight as Mrs. Vanderweide's skirts. Around his neck was a cross large enough to ward off vampires. Perhaps he needed it working with Mrs. Vanderweide. He swept into my room and looked around with an obvious look of distaste. "I've never worked on anything so small. This will take imagination."

This had to stop now. "There's been some mistake..." I began.

Cherry Cobbler

"Now, now, Mrs. Vanderweide told me you'd protest. She said you always do. But that woman has a heart of gold and when she decides to take care of someone, she does so in spite of their financial station."

I just stared, too incredulous to form words.

"We will have to start by replacing that window. It's so eighties."

"Mr., uh, Rolf, I don't want a different window."

He looked at me as if I were a dense child. "I know it's hard to realize that we are so out of date…"

Who was "we"? I tried again. "You don't understand…"

"I'll give you plenty of choices, don't worry."

"No!" I yelled. I was close to grabbing that cross and swinging him around the room.

He looked at me rather shocked. I suppose not too many of his customers yell at him. "I don't want you to decorate my apartment."

"Well! I don't know as if you're in the position to be choosy. I'll have you know I'm the best money can buy around these parts."

"I'm sure you are. I'm sure you're a wonderful decorator."

"Then what seems to be the problem?"

"I like my apartment just the way it is. I didn't ask for a decorator, and I don't want one."

He looked at me as if my nose had grown ten inches, sure that I was lying just like Pinocchio. "Why ever not?"

"I don't know where Mrs. Vanderweide got this idea. I'm sure she meant well, but I don't want anyone decorating my apartment but me."

"Well, I'll have to charge her for the house call anyway. I can't work for free."

"Yes, well, that's reasonable."

"She won't like this."

"Then she should have asked me about it before she just took over. Forcing me to wear her makeup is one thing, redecorating my apartment is quite another."

"Hmm," he said scrutinizing me, probably thinking I needed makeup too. "Very well." And to my relief he left.

My phone rang an hour later. "What do you mean sending Rolf home?" the all too familiar voice asked, sending sparks through the phone.

"Mrs. Vanderweide, I know you meant well but I don't want a decorator. I like my apartment just the way it is," I

Cherry Cobbler

repeated once more, making my voice as determined as possible.

"Well, I never. Of all the ungrateful... To think of turning down Rolf... What are you thinking?" She seemed unable to sustain a whole sentence.

"I'm sorry, Mrs. Vanderweide."

There was a moment of silence, and I didn't know what to suspect. To my surprise, her voice was quite cheerful. "Very well, I'll send my tailor over to design a new wardrobe for you."

"Mrs. Vanderweide, do you really want to do something for me?"

"Of course, darling. I'm certainly trying."

"Then send Rolf to the soup kitchen. They are desperately in need of new facilities. I'm sure he could do wonders there."

I said the right thing. "What a wonderful idea! Our city could be written up as the best soup kitchen in the country. I could call the papers and make sure it was covered by the Associated Press. This will be great publicity, and I can write it off my taxes. You're a genius, Cherry."

"Thank you, Mrs. Vanderweide."

"You're welcome, Cherry. See you Sunday!"

Now that's something I could really look forward to.

30

I called the soup kitchen the next day to warn them. They were delighted, but they hadn't met Rolf yet. He isn't exactly a soup kitchen kind of guy. I hoped that no one hated me when it was all over.

Taking a break at work, I looked up to see Grant walking through the garden center outside my window. I wondered what he was up to since it was a school day, and then I remembered that school had just let out. I waited to see if he would come in to see me, but he never did. It surprised me to realize that I was disappointed.

Around lunchtime I went out to the garden to eat. It was a perfect late spring day so I soaked in the sunshine and smelled the roses that were blooming next to me. My job always allows me to stop and smell the roses, a benefit they should definitely list in the job description.

I stood up to stretch when Grant walked by again, this time carrying a flat of flowers. It had been at least two hours since I'd seen him the last time, so I thought he must be buying enough plants to landscape the White House. I called his name and he waved, never breaking his pace. I hurried to catch up with him. "What in the world are you doing? You've been here for ages."

"Actually only for one morning."

I stared at him as he set the flat of flowers down under a display. Slowly, it dawned on me. "Are you working here?"

He grinned and nodded his head. "I have to take summer jobs to keep busy, or I'd go crazy. I got the idea having lunches here, so I asked if they were hiring. It seems a perfect place to spend the summer."

I smiled back. "It is. I love my job in the summer, even if it is inside. Well, welcome aboard! I guess I'll be seeing you around."

"I don't know if I'll see you much. This job doesn't give many breaks, but I'll try to stop in when I can."

"That will be fun. Maybe we could get Josh and Roslyn to work here, too. It'll be like one big party."

Grant lightly pinched the end of my nose. "I don't think the garden center has a whole lot of need for medical personnel."

"Kill joy!"

"Somebody has to keep you serious."

"Whatever for?"

He laughed. "Good question."

Cherry Cobbler

We both looked awkwardly away, which was strange because we were never awkward around each other. "I'd better get back to work, Cherry blossom."

I blinked as he used my mother's nickname for me. I guess it was a pretty natural place to go for those who spent any amount of time with me. I shrugged my shoulders and put my nose back to the grindstone. Only after one more sniff of the roses, though.

I was just about finished with work, when the phone rang. "Cherry?"

"Yes?"

"This is Sylvia from the soup kitchen."

I smiled to myself as I pictured her in my mind. Sylvia was a sharp African-American woman who ran the kitchen tighter than any captain ever ran a ship. She held the line when finances were tight and rallied the troops when more help was needed. She allowed no nonsense from her volunteers or the customers. Everyone respected her and maybe even feared her a little, myself included. "Hi Sylvia."

"Cherry, what's with this Rolf guy?" Somehow I wasn't too surprised at her tone of voice.

"Ah, you've met Rolf."

"Is he for real?"

"The genuine article."

"I thought characters like him only existed in comedies. He lives in some make believe world that scares me to death."

"Yea, it's a little different than what we're used to dealing with at the kitchen."

"He wants it to look like an Italian villa," she said dryly.

"Hey, Italian's good. I was afraid he'd go for Bohemian or something."

"Cherry, I'm serious. When you said he was coming, I thought he'd help us get some new appliances and serving pieces. This guy wants to tear everything up and start over."

I sighed loud enough to be heard in Cleveland. "I know." I paused, getting my thoughts together. "I think you should throw down some very strict guidelines about leaving your kitchen functional during the entire process, but give him free reign in the decorating part as long as it doesn't stop the kitchen from carrying on."

Sylvia sighed back. "That's what I thought. I don't know, Cherry. I may want to ring his little skinny neck before this is all through."

"I know the feeling."

Cherry Cobbler

"If we didn't need new stuff so bad, I'd send him to Siberia."

"I'd help you."

"Good, just so long as we understand each other."

"Perfectly."

When I hung up the phone, I felt remotely guilty for doing this to Sylvia. I dreaded when the photographers and the press showed up. Then the sparks would really fly. But knowing Sylvia, she'd turn it into a giant recruiting tool for volunteers. If anyone could handle Rolf, it was Sylvia.

When I arrived at the kitchen on Saturday, I couldn't believe my eyes. Rolf had a whole crew of workers there, measuring and figuring out how to knock out walls while keeping the place functional. Every time he talked about doing one more thing, Sylvia glared at him. He seemed to jump a little with each glare, which I was tremendously glad to see. When he saw me, he turned the other way. I wasn't sure whether he was mad at me because I'd rejected the apartment makeover, or if it was because I had gotten him into this job.

We began serving on schedule, thanks to Sylvia's tenacity. All went well until the press came in. What seemed to be a fiasco, Sylvia turned into a recruiting tool, just as I thought. She smiled for the camera and made pleas for help, making it sound like the most fulfilling job in the world. When they left, she walked over to me with clenched teeth. "I'm going to get you for this, Cherry."

I gave my sweetest "I don't know what you are talking about because I'm so innocent" smile, which didn't fool her for a minute. She scowled and I thought for a minute that she was going to slap that smile off my face. I almost ducked.

In the meantime, Gloria had been slinking to the edges, keeping her face off the camera. I didn't know if she was shy or afraid that she was wanted for something. At any rate, I didn't get a chance to talk to her. She'd been avoiding me since the bail. It galled her somehow that I had to be involved.

So I left the kitchen feeling like I was some kind of scourge on the earth. No biblical pestilence had anything on me.

31

I couldn't believe it. Our Bible study had prayed about it and actually decided to take a mission trip to Nigeria to help out Todd. I, who had been so enthusiastic, was the least excited of anyone. I knew then that my attitude had stunk the whole time.

In fact, I said that I wasn't sure I would go, not because I didn't want to go on a mission trip, but because I didn't want to see Todd. I was afraid I'd fall in love all over again and make a mess of things. The others thought I was afraid of the conditions, but Grant knew right away what it was about. In fact, he cornered me after Bible study.

"Is it that you're afraid to see Todd for fear of starting everything up again?"

How was this man so perceptive? "Yea. I'm really over him and I don't want to go through that again."

"Will it help that I'm there?"

What did he mean? How would that help? "What, are you going to punch me or something if you see me get stars in my eyes?"

"No, but I'll be there to talk to."

I looked at him doubtfully.

"Maybe you're over him for good."

"What if I'm not? What if I fall hard?"

Grant looked pained, as if someone had done minor surgery on him. "I'd hate that, Cherry."

"Why would you hate it?"

"Because I can't stand to see you sad. You're all about joy." He reached up and touched my cheek in a way that made me feel warm all over, as if I were the only woman in the world. It made me feel strong and powerful, as if I could conquer anything.

"All right, I'll go, but you have to watch out for me."

Grant's grin looked like Easter. "That's my favorite job in the whole world."

I looked at him and wondered what made him such a nice guy. Too bad he didn't make my blood boil the way Todd did.

There were a million things to do to get ready to go, the hardest of which would be convincing my boss to let me go in the middle of our busiest time at work.

Cherry Cobbler

"Good morning, Mr. Hopkins."

"Good morning, Cherry."

"Could I talk to you a minute?"

"Sure. What's up?"

"You'd better sit down."

He sat on a chair across from me and frowned. "I don't like the sound of that."

"I know. You aren't going to like what I say, but it's really important."

"This is getting worse by the moment."

I took a deep breath and plunged ahead. "I need to take two weeks off to go to Nigeria."

"WHAT?" Poor man. His blood pressure must have gone up several notches. "Whatever for?"

"I'm going on a mission's trip."

"Can't you do that in the winter when we have nothing to do?"

"No, it has to be now. But the good news is that I've found someone to sub for me while I'm gone."

"Who?"

"Mrs. Murphy."

"Mrs. Murphy, our client?"

"The very one."

"Cherry, I love Mrs. Murphy, but does she know anything about the business?"

"Yep, she was a secretary for years and is perhaps the most efficient and normal person I know. You probably won't want me back."

Mr. Hopkins stood up. "Very well."

"Really?" I couldn't believe it could be so easy.

"Yep. You haven't taken a vacation for a long time. We'll manage somehow."

I could have hugged him, but Mr. Hopkins was not the huggable type. "Thank you so much. This means a lot to me."

"When are you leaving?"

"In two weeks."

"Okay, bring Mrs. Murphy in a few days before to show her the ropes."

"I will. Thanks again, Mr. Hopkins."

When I told Sylvia at the soup kitchen where I was going, she was wildly jealous because she'd always wanted to go to Africa. Gloria just snorted when I told her. She still wasn't speaking to me.

I didn't bother to tell Sam and Crystal.

Fortunately, I already had a passport because I'd been on a mission's trip to Costa Rica a few years ago, so nothing was left but the ticket. That took a good chunk out of my savings, but it was for a good cause.

I couldn't believe it. I was going to Africa.

Time flew and before I knew it, I was on a plane to Lagos, Nigeria. Todd had emailed all of us that we would be staying with different families. I was to stay with a couple who attended his church.

As I leaned back and relaxed on the long flight, I tried to absorb myself in the movie that was playing, but it could have been in Greek for all that I made sense of it. My thoughts were spinning like a Ferris wheel gone out of control. For the first time I felt a little bit of panic that perhaps I wasn't prepared for what I was getting into. So in the tradition of Scarlett O'Hara, I decided not to think about that today. I'd think about it tomorrow, and I promptly went to sleep.

After a short layover in London, we were off again. I'd always wanted to see London and now I'd wished we'd planned a day there to see the sights. The three-hour stop only gave me a glimpse of the wonderful, old-fashioned cabs the city is famous for. Other than that, it looked pretty much like any other airport.

By the time we arrived in Lagos, my days and nights were turned around. We'd left the USA at four o'clock in the afternoon, and it was now two o'clock in the afternoon in Nigeria, but my body clock was at about four o'clock in the morning. I felt like I did in college when I pulled all-nighters right before a big exam, usually leaving me too tired to remember a thing I'd studied.

So in that muzzle-brained frame of mind, I started our two-week adventure.

Todd was waiting for us, looking like a schoolboy who was about to get the whole summer off. He greeted me with a hug, along with everyone else. I was relieved to realize that the hug didn't make my heart do flip-flops, and I knew that I was reading the situation realistically. I noticed Grant watching me as we walked to the baggage claim. It was as if he was staring at a piece of crystal that was about to be dropped on a tile floor. I smiled to relieve him and it worked. His whole face relaxed.

My bag finally came around the turnstile, looking a little more beat up than when I'd packed it. Todd's eyebrows rose at the size of it; I had to admit, it looked like it could hold a small horse. But Grant took it off the conveyor belt and whispered a prayer of thanks that it had wheels.

When we got outside, I realized that this was warmth and humidity that even the US Midwest knew nothing about. With all the fumes of cars, cabs, and buses, I felt as if I was gasping for air.

Todd moved us to an old yellow bus that was actually a large van. It had been dented in nearly every part of its outside anatomy so that it looked as if it had been decorated that way on purpose. There were so many people already inside that the bus bowed in the middle. I shot a glance of apprehension at Todd, but evidently he didn't seem to think it was cause for concern. We squeezed in, ignoring glances of disgust at the size of my suitcase.

The only good thing about the bus was that the driver played cheerful music, which reminded me of Jamaican or Calypso music. It was jovial and lively, making me smile in spite of my fear of falling through the floor when the bus broke in two.

Todd explained that we were heading out to the suburbs, which gave me hope. Suburbs were always nicer than cities and so far, the city seemed nice. There were high-rises everywhere and the highway system seemed well maintained, although everyone drove like maniacs, honking their horns continuously.

There were billboards everywhere, advertising brands I was quite familiar with and some I'd never heard of. At one point, I saw a beautiful cathedral that looked as if it had been there for several centuries. I hoped that I'd get to see inside it sometime.

As we left the city proper and entered the suburbs, my heart sank. The farther out we got, the more run down and decrepit everything appeared. Most homes and businesses were in disrepair and poverty was evident everywhere, but I breathed in deeply and renewed my commitment. After all, missionaries have had to face much worse.

I began to enjoy the unique things I was seeing. Brightly costumed women walked by carrying large baskets full of produce on their heads. A vacant lot held so many signs that no one could possibly read them all. Merchants, without the luxury of a building, hawked their wares at every street corner. Open-air markets overflowed with enticing goods. Spices filled the air with their aroma. Older children played in the streets with makeshift soccer balls, and little ones around the legs of their parents as they shopped.

My stop was first at a modest, two-story home that had once been painted a bright blue but had now faded to a dusty color. In better repair than many of the homes in the area, it bloomed with flowers that had been lovingly tended. We went up the rickety steps and knocked on the door. A rather tall, slender woman answered the

Cherry Cobbler

door, throwing her arms open wide, "You must be Cherry! Welcome to our home. I'm Ruth, by the way."

I liked Ruth immediately. She was very dark skinned which made her smile seem twice as brilliant. Her face was not beautiful, but rather what my grandmother would have called handsome. Her personality was as bright as the intense Nigerian sun and her accent lilting.

"Don't just stand there, come in, come in." Her eyes widened a bit when she saw my suitcase, but she recovered quickly. "My, you do look as if you intend to stay a while. I like a woman who is prepared."

I loved her for that comment.

32

Ruth showed me to a functional room that had a twin bed with a brightly colored bedspread. She explained that it was her son's room who was away at college. "We're glad the room is open right now. We usually have a child we're caring for staying with us, but all is peaceful among our relatives right now." I thanked her for taking me in, squeezed my suitcase through the door (just barely) and made my way around the little bit of floor space that was left.

Todd left me, explaining that he needed to drop the others off to their homes and that he'd be back to gather us all together in a few hours. I watched him leave and felt that I wanted nothing more than to lie down and go to sleep.

But, alas, it was not to be. "So, Cherry, sit down and tell me all about yourself."

I obeyed. "Well, there's not much to tell. I work at a garden center back home." This took some explaining because Nigeria didn't have garden centers. It was beyond Ruth's imagination that someone would pay

Cherry Cobbler

someone to map out their yard for them. She shook her head and went on to the next question.

"So, how did you meet Todd?"

"We were in a Bible study together."

"Ah, a wonderful place to meet someone. How long have you been engaged?"

"Oh! We're not engaged."

Ruth looked as if I'd told her that I wasn't a woman. "What do you mean? Todd told me you were."

"He did?"

"Yes. He said that he was going to marry you; that he hoped you'd be married by the end of the two weeks that you're here."

I felt my face getting hot. In fact, my whole body felt as if I were put in a microwave. I wanted to say something, but my words were stuck somewhere behind my windpipe, and I was having trouble breathing. Ruth noticed. "Are you all right?"

I nodded, still unable to speak.

"I'll get you some water." And she disappeared into the kitchen. I had strict orders from everyone not to drink the water, so I wasn't sure what to do, but when she handed me that glass, I guzzled it down, defying those parasites to get me. Then Ruth took the glass from me, sat down beside me and took my hand. "You'd better tell me what you're thinking. I have a feeling you're going to need someone to talk to while you're here."

I was relieved to find I hadn't been struck dumb after all. "Are you sure that's what Todd said?

"Pretty sure."

"You couldn't be mistaken?"

"No. I'm sure that's what he said. Don't you like Todd?"

How ironic. "Of course I like him, but I had no idea he felt that way about me."

She grinned and patted my hand the way a mother would assure her child. "He's very fond of you – in fact, he's talked of little else since he returned."

"Well, this is the first I've heard of it." I rung my hands and looked around the room. "You know, I think I need to lie down. I'm so tired."

Ruth jumped up. "Silly me, you must be exhausted. I forgot about how your days and nights must be mixed up. You go rest, and I'll work on dinner."

I walked into the little room, took my shoes off and fell into a deep sleep where I dreamed of a heaven where no decisions had to be made.

Cherry Cobbler

I awoke to Todd standing over me. He startled me so much that I screamed. Ruth and a man I didn't know came running into the bedroom. I would have laughed if I'd been able to absorb my surroundings. The three of them were standing shoulder to shoulder, looking as if they'd been stuffed in a toy box for Christmas morning, due to the fact that my suitcase took up the whole room. "Law, child, what on earth is the matter?" Ruth asked.

"I'm sorry. I was sound asleep and not really awake yet when I saw Todd. It scared me."

It was then that I noticed that Todd looked like a wild-eyed mongoose about to bolt. It gave me the giggles, which caused everyone else to begin laughing.

"By the way, this is my husband, Mathias."

Mathias was shorter than Ruth with lighter skin and had the longest, most serious face I'd ever seen. The poor man looked as if he'd seen Armageddon that very day. But he was proper British, polite, and held himself with a dignity I'd rarely seen. He gave a little bow and said, "Welcome to our home, Cherry," with a delightful accent that made me feel that I was listening to a dramatic radio program.

"Thank you for letting me stay. I'll try not to scream anymore." Mathias gave the faintest of smiles at that comment, but Ruth laughed out loud, "Come on. Dinner's getting cold."

Todd went on, saying he was going to check on the others. I felt relieved to see him go. For some reason I couldn't understand, I felt desperate to talk to Grant.

Dinner was simple but hearty. Mathias spoke only when directly addressed, but Ruth kept things lively the entire time. "Do you know what I did this morning?"

We all looked at her, but she didn't wait for an answer. "I chased a pig." With that declaration, she leaned back, crossed her arms and waited for the questions. Mathias just stared at her, but I took the bait. "Why?"

"I'm glad you asked!" she cried as if amazed at the question. "Because a child was bringing it to the market to sell, and it got away."

"How big was it?" I was getting curious now.

"Oh about so big," and she put her arms about two feet apart.

"A little guy."

Ruth chuckled, "Little but strong. Have you ever tried to grab a squirming pig that's trying to get away?"

Of course, I hadn't. But before I could answer, Mathias said in his slow, methodical voice, "Everyone has, Ruth."

Cherry Cobbler

I raised my eyebrows, and Ruth seized on it at once. "Ah see, Cherry hasn't! Anyway, it began running through the market place, squealing, well, like a pig." She laughed heartily at her own joke and continued, "I chased that thing for five blocks, grabbing it but then having to let go because it squirmed. Others were trying to catch it too, but I was afraid they would keep it instead of giving it back to the boy, so I tried harder. Anyway, I finally cornered it, and do you know how I caught it?"

Again, it was up to me. "How?"

"I threw a basket over it, then it began running with that basket on top of it. Oh, you should've seen it," she howled. "It was quite a sight. Finally it ran smack into the side of a building, knocking it silly. I just picked it up and took it back to the boy, who was frantic. I imagine he would have gotten quite a whooping for losing a pig." Ruth smiled and looked around for approval from her audience.

"You must have been exhausted after all that running."

She winked, "I'm in pretty good shape for being an old one," and she laughed again. Dinner with Ruth was going to be fun.

After dinner, Todd came by again. I offered to help with dishes, but Ruth shooed us away, "You two go on. Leave the work to me. You'll have plenty of other times to help." She watched us walk off with a worried look in her eye.

We'd just rounded a corner when I heard a voice say, "Hey you, you're mighty pretty!" It was an odd sounding voice, kind of squawky, and I looked every which way but could spot no one. Todd seemed a little nervous too. We took a few more steps when the same voice said, "How about a kiss?"

I swung around but even though there were several people about, none looked as though they matched the voice. We both walked on when we heard, "Come with me!" Todd looked around, wondering what might happen when we heard a young boy begin giggling and pointing at us. On his arm was a parrot.

"You thought Sweetie was a person, didn't you?" and he petted the bird and whispered praise to her.

"Did you teach her all those sentences?"

He shook his head. "No, my big brother did. He likes to tease the girls."

"Well, be careful you don't get slapped, young man."

The boy looked offended at such a suggestion and took off in the other direction, the bird calling, "Bye now!" as they went.

Cherry Cobbler

Todd and I laughed, relieved to have something break the tension. It gave me the courage to speak. "Todd, Ruth thinks we're engaged."

He looked surprised, to my relief. "She does?"

All the fun I'd felt about the parrot melted away. "Why would she think that?"

He shrugged his shoulders.

"I came here to do mission work, that's all." I couldn't believe I was saying this. A few months ago, I thought I'd follow this man anywhere. Todd looked as if someone had let the wind out of his sails. "I thought…" he stopped and looked away as if hoping to find the words written in the sky. "I thought since you came, that meant…" and his voice drifted.

"That meant I was interested in a relationship?"

"Yea."

"Wouldn't it have made sense to talk to me about it first?"

He looked uncomfortable, as if someone had released a colony of ants in his shirt. "Hopefully, in the next couple of weeks we'll both know whether we want to pursue a relationship." He kicked a stone with his shoe, sending it flying across the road until it hit a poor starved dog standing in the street. It yelped. I felt like yelping too.

Unexpectedly he smiled. "You might not want to go back. You certainly brought enough stuff to stay for good." His grin grew even wider. I hit him. He yelped. We were a yelping bunch.

33

The next morning, we divided into teams of three to visit Todd's AIDS patients. Todd made sure I was in his group, and I made sure Grant was the third person. I felt like using him as a shield. I was more than a little nervous. I was also a bit terrified about visiting the patients. I'd only known one person with AIDS, an elderly man who had attended our Bible study. When he became really ill, he moved to Texas with his brother so I'd never had to see him at his worst.

The first home we came to was poorly cared for. The yard was dirt with nothing growing anywhere near it, and the house looked as if it were on its last legs; that one strong wind would knock it down.

Inside was even worse. The dirty dishes were covered with flies, and the floor looked as though it hadn't been swept in weeks. There were a couple of children playing with a mangy looking dog, but most startling was the person in the bed. This woman looked as if she was ninety, but Todd later told us she was forty. The children were her grandchildren; their mother had died a few years ago. Their father had died before they really had a chance to know him.

The poor woman looked as if she were a skeleton with skin stretched over her. All muscle tone had left a long time ago, making it impossible for her to get out of bed. Todd immediately went over to her, sat down, and began reading Scripture and praying with her. I looked around the room and tried to make myself useful. I set down the food that Todd had brought, washed the dishes, and swept the floor.

Todd was still muttering things to the woman, so Grant decided to concentrate on the children. He walked over and sat down next to them. They looked at him warily.

"What's your dog's name?"

"Moses," said the boy, who was the oldest.

"Wow! Quite a name for a dog."

"He's a big dog," the girl said indignantly.

Grant quickly agreed, "But not as big as an elephant." That got them both laughing. "Do you want to hear a joke about an elephant?"

Each head bobbed up and down.

"Why did the elephant paint his toenails red?"

They giggled before he could even get to the punch line. "So he could hide in the cherry tree." Now they laughed so hard, they held their sides, encouraging him to go on.

Cherry Cobbler

"How do you know when there is an elephant under your bed?" Two faces looked at him, waiting to be entertained. "When your nose touches the ceiling."

Peals of laughter filled the little house. I knew only one elephant joke, so I decided to jump in. "What time is it when an elephant sits on the fence?" By this time they had climbed up into Grant's lap, both ready to adopt him permanently. "Time to fix the fence!" They both chuckled so vigorously that they fell off his lap and rolled on the floor. I'd never had such a responsive audience.

I was just wondering what to follow it up with, when I felt a hand on my shoulder. "Let's go, Cherry, Grant. We have others to see."

I noticed a look on Todd's face that I didn't like. I wondered what it meant. I didn't have to wonder for long. As soon as we were outside, I found out. "What were you doing?" he asked.

"Well, I did the dishes and swept the floor…"

"You know that's not what I'm talking about."

Grant added, "You mean the elephant jokes?"

He just nodded, with his arms folded in front of him, looking like my grandfather when he used to scold me for getting into his tools.

"I was just trying to entertain the kids," Grant said with a grin. "They looked as though they hadn't had a moment of fun in quite a while."

Todd's voice raised a few notches. "I was there to help their grandmother. The kids aren't sick. We could hardly talk because of all the racket you were making."

Now I was getting mad. "The kids need help too. What about their future?"

"Well, elephant jokes sure aren't going to help their future."

"They might," I said indignantly. "They might be just what they need to get them through a tough day."

"Oh Cherry, that's ridiculous."

I was so mad at this point, that I couldn't talk about it anymore. Todd evidently thought he'd won, so he went on. "Now in this next house, just be quiet and listen. You might learn something."

Right now the only thing I wanted to learn was how to give a quick left hook. I felt like stomping off when I caught Grant's eye. His eyes were wide and his eyebrows high, with the distinctive look of trying to hold back a chuckle. It brought me the relief I needed.

Cherry Cobbler

Fortunately there were no children at the next house to tempt me. But I also felt useless and more than a little depressed. This house needed cleaning too, which I diligently applied myself to, banging things around more loudly than necessary. I already knew I wanted to go home.

Because I'd finished what I was doing and Todd was still meeting with the man we'd come to see, I wandered outside and sat on the stoop, watching people pass as my thoughts spun, God what am I doing here? I am such an idiot. How can you possibly love me? My gaze rested on a young man on a bicycle peddling by. When he was out of sight, I looked down. Gazing up at me was the most beautiful lizard I'd ever seen. It had a bright red head, a blue body, and its hind legs and tail were turquoise. He looked so intelligent that I almost expected him to start talking to me like out of some Disney movie. We looked at each other for several minutes and then he took off toward the alley that ran by the house. I watched him go and felt that he'd surely been sent to reassure me. If God can use a donkey, he certainly can use a redheaded lizard!

Grant had been doing some cleaning too, but now he came out to sit beside me. "How ya' doin'?" he asked in his lazy, relaxing tone of voice. It lifted my spirits further.

"Okay. It's just that I haven't been scolded so severely in a while."

"Yea, I guess that's my fault. I'm sorry I got you in trouble."

"Are you kidding? You were great with those kids. I loved watching you."

"They were awfully cute. Elephant jokes are universal." He picked up some pebbles and threw them a ways into the street. "How are you doing around Todd?"

I didn't want to tell him about Todd's romantic interest in me, so I ignored that part. "Okay."

"Really?"

"Yea. I mean he's attractive and all that, but it's different seeing him again. I definitely had rose-colored glasses on before."

Grant looked at me hopefully, "No kidding? That's a great thing to realize."

I had to agree.

When Todd came out, I was in a better mood. We walked to a small café for lunch and enjoyed a pleasant meal with the others. Everyone wanted to talk about their experiences except for Grant and me. We shared the kind of bond that two kids in detention together feel. Todd wanted us to go with him on the rest of his rounds, but I'd had enough for one day. I told him I'd walk back to Ruth's

Cherry Cobbler

house and take a nap. He accepted that, and we parted ways. I looked back and saw Grant watching me with concern in his eyes.

As I was walking, I came across an open-air market. I'd seen several since I'd been here, but hadn't been able to wander around in one. I did so now, stopping to buy presents for my family and friends. I purchased lots of spices for my mom, bright fabric for Mrs. Murphy to thank her for helping me out, a carved deer for my dad, and carved pens for Roslyn, Josh, Grant, Sam and Crystal. At the last minute, I bought a large bouquet of flowers for Ruth and Mathias. I left the market whistling, enjoying myself for the first time since I'd arrived.

I presented Ruth with the flowers and showed her all my other presents, which she politely exclaimed over. She seemed truly delighted with the flowers, a luxury she could rarely indulge in. After all that, I finally got the nap I needed so badly.

I awoke around dinnertime and found Todd waiting. I joyfully showed him all the gifts I'd bought, but he only frowned. "You spent time shopping instead of helping with the AIDS patients? That's pretty selfish, Cherry."

I looked at Ruth and she looked away, obviously refusing to take sides. I simply threw my arms up, and in my very chicken way, offered to help with dinner so that I could avoid talking about it at all. Thankfully Ruth accepted my offer.

As we chopped vegetables and talked cheerfully, I was steaming so much inside that I was surprised that the food wasn't cooked before it ever made it to the stove.

After dinner, we all got ready to go to church for the midweek service. I thought of the beautiful cathedral we'd passed and wondered what the church would look like. It almost certainly would be different than my church at home that the casual observer would think was a theater.

We took a bus to get there. It ended up taking about twenty minutes with lots of stops, starts and swerves. Road travel in Nigeria is good for one's prayer life.

When we got out, I saw an enormous sign that advertised the church. In fact, the sign was so large that I couldn't see the church behind it. Walking around the billboard, I caught a glimpse of the storefront building that housed the church. Like my church at home, nothing on the outside gave away the fact that this was a house of worship.

Inside was more promising. Banners of all shapes and sizes decorated the walls, and men and women alike were dressed in colorful choir robes. There was a buzz of excitement at being together to celebrate knowing God. I marveled that I could come halfway around the world and feel such a deep connection with people. It was a tiny glimpse of what it will be like in heaven.

Cherry Cobbler

When the service began, I felt I was holding on for dear life. The people sang with enthusiasm, as if their life depended on it. They cried out to God in praise and petition, lifting their voices to the very heavens.

The pastor spoke with power and conviction. No microphone was needed because his voice thundered through the little storefront until the windows shook. I thought if I were hiding some sin that I'd not want to sit under his preaching. I don't know how Gabriel himself could outdo this guy in the shock and awe department.

When it was over, we were smothered in welcome, feeling that we were long-lost sisters and brothers who'd just found our way home. Jeannie and her husband glowed in the fellowship. It was fun seeing how well they adapted to the new environment. I went home with Ruth and Mathias. I felt so exhausted on the ride home that I was afraid I'd fall asleep. I wasn't sure if I still had jet lag or if all the emotion of the service had drained me. Either way, I hit my pillow like a torpedo.

The next day, we had meetings all morning with Bible study, prayer, and singing. I felt relieved. It meant I didn't have to face any more AIDS patients or worse, Todd's disapproval of what I did wrong.

So I spent the morning writing Roslyn. I started it and wadded it up at least ten times. Finally I settled on the following:

Dear Roslyn,

I've arrived safely and am trying to catch up on my sleep. Nigeria is hot as you know what, but the hearts are warm too. Last night we went to a church service which was the liveliest I'd ever been to. The children were all captivated; no one had to shush them because they hung on every moment of it.

Yesterday I also went with Todd to visit his patients. I only saw two of them, but I don't think I understood what suffering was until I saw them. One man told Todd that all he wanted was to be home with the Lord in his mansion of glory. He wanted Todd to read that part in the Bible over and over again. "Imagine," he said, "that Jesus would have a whole mansion ready just for me." When people have so little, they long for heaven a lot more than we do.

The children make me the saddest. Grant tried to cheer up a couple of them. They particularly liked his elephant jokes. Todd wasn't so crazy about them though.

Todd seems a little different than I remember him. He was lighter and more fun at home when he didn't have all the pressure of ministry on him. He's good at what he does and takes it seriously. Oh man, does he take it seriously! He makes me feel like he's Mother Theresa and I'm Ronald MacDonald. I'm not sure what to do about it (not just the gender confusion in my analogy either).

Cherry Cobbler

Anyway, it's only the second day and we have lots more adventures coming. Thanks for being such a great friend. I miss you.

Love,

Cherry

I looked at the letter and sighed. Only two days gone out of two weeks. It already felt like life in prison without parole.

34

Todd surprised us the next day by packing a picnic to take to the beach. See, I told myself, things are picking up. You just needed to give it a chance. What could be more romantic than a picnic lunch?

The beach was beautiful. I kicked off my shoes and waded in the surf. Grant jumped right in and did various porpoise imitations, which had us all holding our sides with laughter. Todd came as close as he could without getting his feet wet. "Take your shoes off and wade in," I said, "It's great."

He shook his head and smiled. "I don't really like it when the sand sticks all over me after my feet get wet."

"Suit yourself, but you're missing a lot."

He nodded and was clearly not to be persuaded, but at least he didn't seem to mind that I was doing it.

After a while we all drifted back to the blanket he'd brought, and he proudly spread out the lunch he'd carefully made. I sat on the edge of the blanket so that I wouldn't get my sandy feet on it since that seemed to be a problem.

Cherry Cobbler

The lunch was great. Todd had carefully prepared egg salad sandwiches, potato salad, and a wonderful fresh fruit salad. We all raved about it.

"Yea, I've got the recipes all written out so when my future wife does it, it will taste just the same. It's all in the exact amounts I use."

I stared at him to see if he was serious and when I realized he was, I almost lost my appetite, which is saying a lot for me.

When we weren't talking about sand, food, or elephant jokes, Todd and I were able to have an enjoyable conversation. We both agreed that we loved Ruth and Mathias, and that the church service was great. We both liked the outdoor market, although Todd thought I should stick to buying only necessities, and we both thought that June in Nigeria is too hot.

After that, we seemed out of things to talk about so I got up and waded in the water again. Grant joined me. "Are you okay, Cherry? Something seems to be going on that I don't know about. Is Todd interested in you? He looked at you after that 'future wife' remark as though he had you in mind."

How did he do that? Grant was definitely the most perceptive man I'd ever met. "Okay," I gave in. "He is interested in me."

Grant nodded without shock or surprise. "The roles have reversed." Then he looked closely at me. "Or are you interested?"

"He doesn't seem the same. I'd made him into something else in my mind."

Grant nodded again, with no hint of scolding. He was a great friend.

On the bus trip back, Todd made sure he sat by me. Looking for common ground, I asked him about his friends. "Who are they? Who do you hang out with when you have free time?"

He looked as if I'd asked if he gambled on the weekends. "I don't really have a lot of free time. The work I do is pretty all consuming. That's why I wanted you to come, I guess. Someone to help me in my work so that it wouldn't be so exhausting."

I frowned deeply, hoping he noticed. "Todd, do you want me here just to be a worker?"

"Oh no, of course not! I could ask the mission board to send someone else for that." He looked down and twisted his hands nervously. Words didn't come easily for him. "No, I want someone who understands my work, who feels passion for the same things I do. Someone I can talk to and find strength with as we sacrifice together."

Cherry Cobbler

"Is it all work and sacrifice?"

"Mostly. Not much else in life has meaning."

I fell quiet and stared ahead. I didn't know if I could live a life that was all work and sacrifice. I liked elephant jokes too much. Why would God make me love elephant jokes and then never let me tell them? It was truly a theological question for the ages. See, I couldn't even think about work and sacrifice without finding some humor in it. Somehow the whole train of thought made me think about Grant. He would love such a discussion.

Back at Ruth's things seemed lighter. I was sure Ruth would like just about any kind of joke. She was a barrel of fun. I volunteered to cook dinner that night. "Ooo, I'd be pleased as a chameleon to get out of cooking for a night," Ruth pronounced.

I told her I'd run to the market and purchase some things to cook. She just sunk into her chair and smiled.

The market was bustling with activity. I bought some fresh fish, some vegetables I recognized, and some fruit I didn't. I also bought a big loaf of bread.

Fortunately, Ruth had spices that I knew and flour and milk. I baked the fish with chives, garlic and olive oil and made a white sauce for the vegetables. I cut the fruit into a salad and cooked some rice with chives and peppers.

Then I smothered the bread in more oil and garlic. It was good we weren't going anywhere tonight. Our breath would only be suitable if we were around each other.

The meal was a great hit and Ruth enjoyed sitting again while I did dishes. She entertained me with more stories. "Do you know what my mother and I used to do every Christmas?"

I looked up with a question in my eyes, thinking I'd hear about some recipe or decoration. "We used to cook food for 300 people, then take it to the poor side of town and serve it until it was gone."

My mouth almost hit the dishwater. "You cooked for 300 people?" I'd never cooked for more than twelve.

She nodded. "My mother always said that we had so much that we needed to share it with others."

"What a wonderful mom."

"She was a saint. I'm sure her reward in heaven is great." Ruth became sad for the first time since I'd met her. She changed the subject. "So, how are you and Todd getting along?"

I made a slight face, which she noticed. "That good, huh," she said dryly.

"No, I'm glad you asked. It's not working out."

"Do you want to talk about it?"

Cherry Cobbler

I nodded as I wiped the last dish and sat down next to her. "Todd doesn't seem to have much of a sense of humor."

I don't know what Ruth expected, but not that. She laughed out loud. "Good grief. Is that all?"

"No," I said reluctantly, a little afraid to go on. She took care of that.

"I'm sorry. I told you to talk to me and then made fun of you. Go on. I won't do it again."

"Thanks." I tried to collect my thoughts so it wouldn't just come down to Todd not liking my jokes. "It's just that I want to be with someone I enjoy and who enjoys me. He seems to find fault in everything I do. I kind of get the feeling that no matter how hard I try, I'll disappoint him."

"Hmm. That's serious. We women need to feel that our men can't get on without us, not that they want to change us. That's always been the woman's job!"

"That's what I thought! It's good to hear you say it, though. I was afraid I was being selfish."

"No, if you feel that way now, it will be ten times worse after you get married. Have you talked to Todd about it?"

"Uh, no."

"Well, that's where you need to start. First thing tomorrow, you two need to have a talk."

I got up and hugged Ruth. "Thank you. I'm sure glad that God made sure I stayed with you. He knew I was going to need your wisdom."

"I don't know about that! I've never claimed wisdom, just good old common sense."

"Just what I often lack," I said with an exaggerated stage sigh.

"Shoot. You're full of common sense." Then she looked at me sideways and grinned wickedly, "You just don't always know it."

I smiled back and snapped my towel at her.

35

The next day Todd came to get me to see his patients. As soon as we went out the door, I spoke up. "Todd, we have to talk."

"Okay, we can talk as we go."

"No, this is important. It's the sitting and talking kind of important, not the walking and talking kind."

He shrugged his shoulders, "All right, how long is this going to take?"

"It doesn't matter if it takes all day. It's something we have to hash out."

"I don't understand."

"I know. That's just it."

"What?"

"Todd, I think we are on different pages."

"Different pages of what?"

It was like talking to a person with a learning disability. "You're right. Maybe we're on whole different books."

Todd had it with my analogies. "Get to the point, Cherry. What's this about?"

I decided to be blunt. "You need to know that there is no future in our relationship. You're not making me happy, and I'm certainly not making you happy."

"Yes, you are. I love having you here."

"How can you say that?"

"It's great having someone to talk to, to share things with," he paused as if looking for more eloquent words but ended with, "to do things with."

"But that's just it. We aren't really talking, sharing, and doing. We're going through the motions, but I don't feel that I've connected with you at all."

"What do you mean, Cherry? We've talked about work and about the things we like…" He stopped because even he realized there was nothing else to say.

"We've talked about your work and what you like. You haven't listened to what kind of work I want to do or what I like at all."

Now I'd made him mad. The way his face was turning kind of purple was a real tip off. "I've listened to you. Back in the US, you spent hours telling me about how you wanted to be a missionary. I believed you!"

Cherry Cobbler

At that I felt a great pang of guilt. Of course he believed me. He wouldn't suspect that I was just making all that up to get a date. In his realm, such a woman didn't exist. But I did exist, and it was time to come clean. "Todd, I never in my life wanted to be a missionary until I met you. And even then I mostly liked the idea of being your wife, not doing the work. I kind of hoped that you'd let me do my own thing while you did yours."

He stared at me as if I'd slapped him. "You lied to me?" The way he said it was pitiful, the way a five-year-old would say it to his mother.

"I lied to myself. I convinced myself that I wanted to be a missionary because I was so attracted to you."

Todd put his head in his hands and looked down. He tried to make eye contact with me once in the next few minutes, but he couldn't sustain it. I thought maybe I'd have to abandon the idea of any response at all, but finally he spoke, "I can't believe it. You're not the woman I thought you were. I don't even know you."

I felt relieved that he got it, even if it hurt us both. "No, you don't, and I didn't really know you because I'd never seen you at work, which is obviously your life."

He nodded. "What did you want your life to look like if you married me?"

"I mostly wanted to be a wife to you, to be a companion and friend and to ease your load."

"How could you do that without helping me in my work?"

"Well, I thought by bringing cheer and laughter to your work, but you don't seem to want that."

"It just doesn't seem to fit."

I nodded. There seemed nothing else to say.

He waited and when I had nothing to add, he offered. "I'm going to see a patient who is in the early stages of AIDS. I'm going to instruct him on what to expect. What do you want to do?"

I was delighted with the question and told him so, "Thank you for asking! Does he have children?"

"No, but he has a wife and sister."

"Can I tell them jokes?"

Todd threw his arms up in exasperation. "Isn't there anything else you can think of to do?"

"Not really."

"What about reading Scripture to them and praying?"

"I could do that, as long as I did it my way. Fair enough?"

"I guess so." Those were his words, but he looked pretty doubtful. At least he was willing to let me try.

Cherry Cobbler

Grant joined us, to my relief, and we arrived at the humble home within a few minutes. This man was in pretty good shape. He hadn't started losing weight yet and his wife and sister kept the place spic and span. It was a relief to see things appear normal, but I knew they were facing the kinds of things I'd seen in the more advanced stages. It made me sad.

But as Todd and Grant sat down with the man, I asked the women if we could talk outside. They looked at me curiously, but agreed. I asked them if they had a Bible, which they did. Turning to the twenty-third Psalm, I read it to them, saying, "You may know this Scripture well, but it will be a great comfort to you as things get harder with your husband and brother. Let's talk about what it means. It says the Lord—that's Jesus—is my shepherd. We need a shepherd, because we are just dumb sheep." At this their eyebrows went up. Clearly they thought this white woman had lost her marbles, but I had their attention.

"As I said, sheep are dumb. They can't even find water without their shepherd, and they are also helpless and liable to get attacked at any moment. We're just like that. We need Jesus for the simplest, everyday things. Otherwise, we can't even meet our daily needs, and we will be attacked by Satan and be discouraged.

"I grew up in the country and saw sheep regularly. Do you know that once when a farmer I knew burned a big pile of rubbish, his sheep walked right into it, trying to figure out what was going on? It wasn't until he chased them away that they backed off. Otherwise they would have suffocated themselves. Isn't that just like us? We are so curious about the things of the world that in our ignorance, we put our faces right in the smoke until we can't breathe. You will need to be careful not to do that when your loved one gets ill. You'll need to listen to your shepherd and let him lead you out of the smoke into the green pastures."

I stopped talking and looked at them. They smiled. The younger one said, "You explained that really well. I'll remember it and think about it when things get hard." The older one nodded a little dubiously.

"Can I pray with you?"

They both nodded. I took their hands and prayed for the Shepherd to keep them close through the days ahead. Just as I'd finished, Todd and Grant came out. "Ready?"

"Yes, I'm ready." I waved goodbye and the smiling women waved back. I wasn't sure whether they were smiling because they liked me, or because they were glad to get rid of me.

"Any jokes?" Todd asked.

"No, just some fun examples from my childhood."

He raised his eyebrows. "Do you think it helped?"

"I have no idea. At least I don't think I did any damage."

Cherry Cobbler

"Well, there's something to be said for that." He tried to smile, but he looked a little nervous. I couldn't blame him. Grant looked at us curiously, wondering what that was all about. I just winked at him, bringing a smile to his face. I was so glad he was here.

The next patient was again at the throes of death. She had children, but I'd learned my lesson. Grant and I took them outside and told elephant jokes. I couldn't help but think it would help their mother to hear them laugh in the distance.

Over lunch, we talked about the patients. "How do you keep from becoming discouraged, Todd?" Jeannie asked. "I mean, these people aren't going to get better."

"I know. It can get hard, but I feel my job is to get them ready for the next life, which gives them hope that no miracle cure could."

"That's wonderful," I added. He must have been getting gun-shy about my comments because he looked at me with a question in his eyes. "No, I mean it. I think what you do is wonderful." I grew quiet and added, "But I don't know if I could keep perspective doing this day after day."

He nodded and we moved to other subjects after that, but my statement of fact was a shadow over everything. We both knew the answer.

36

I looked for some time to talk to Grant and found it the next day. For some reason I felt desperate to get his take on things. "Are you glad we came?" I asked.

"Yes, I am. It's a beautiful country with warm people, and I feel privileged to have a small part. What about you?"

"I think now that I've settled some things with Todd, I can enjoy myself. I can't believe what an idiot I was when he was in the US. He's not even attractive to me now."

"So, it's great you came. You can now close this chapter of your life with no regrets."

"Yea. It's a relief." I looked at him and felt like giving him a hug, but I restrained myself. "I'm sure glad you came."

"Me too," he smiled like the good friend he was.

"By the way, I've been meaning to ask you. Do you think that God can use elephant jokes for His glory?"

Grant laughed out loud. "Absolutely! Were you having doubts?"

"Some. I have to admit that Todd seems to think that our gifts and personalities are pretty worthless."

"Todd's a great guy, and God made him just right to help these people. But He uses us too, even with our quirkiness."

I smiled. "We are quirky, aren't we? But in a good way."

"In a very good way." Grant looked away smiling. "For instance, when you laugh, I see God's glory all over the place."

"Really?"

"Yep. You reflect Him all the time. He made you full of His joy and it can't help but spill over. I'm a better person knowing you."

"You're a nice guy, Grant."

"Yea, you're spilling over with joy and I'm spilling over with niceness. Kind of sickening isn't it?"

"Very!" It was great knowing exactly what he meant.

After that day, Todd and I got along a lot better. He still didn't get my jokes or understand my approach to life, and I couldn't fathom how seriously he took everything. In fact, we found out we were as opposite as people could be, and that we really didn't have a single thing in common. It was as if we'd worked out a companionship that allowed us to work together but other than that, there was nothing.

Cherry Cobbler

He hugged me once after a day's work. It felt like a hug my brother gave me when my mother said we had to hug and make up; purely functional, no emotion.

By the middle of the second week, there was no doubt. Right before we went to church, Todd took my hands in his, gazed directly into my eyes and said, "There is no way in the world this is going to work, Cherry."

I almost laughed. I'd waited my whole life for a man to take my hands and gaze into my eyes and now it was happening. How ironic. But he was waiting for a response. "I know," was all I managed to spit out.

"I'm sorry that I put you through all of this."

"No, I started the whole thing, so if anyone is to blame, it's me."

He smiled just a little and said, "That's true."

I hit him lightly and smiled back. "I am glad I came though. I'll remember these people for a long time to come and pray for them and for your ministry to them."

"Thanks, Cherry. I appreciate that."

And with those few words, it was over.

With the few days we had left, Grant and I spent them revisiting some of our favorite patients, taking the children and women gifts. I also took Ruth shopping and bought her some much needed items for her household. Leaving her would be the worst part about going back to the US. In two short weeks, she'd become a second mother.

We had a great heart to heart talk. "I'm sorry it didn't work out between you two, Cherry."

"I'm not."

"What?" Ruth was quick, but even she had trouble following my train of thought.

"It became so clear to me that we aren't right for each other that I can't even be sorry – just glad that neither of us did something we'd regret."

She nodded. "So what went wrong?"

"No one thing. It was more like everything. We had nothing in common. Each of us pretended the other was the person we wanted without really getting to know the persons we were."

Ruth looked slightly confused. "I think I followed that. So what will you do now?"

I sighed too deeply. It made her frown. "I guess I'll just go back to being a secretary and settle in to the single life again. I need a break from falling in love."

Cherry Cobbler

She nodded. "I can see how that would be necessary. You're welcome to stay with Mathias and me indefinitely if you want a change."

I hugged her and cried.

On the flight home Grant sat next to me as if guarding me from the cares of life. I leaned on his shoulder and fell asleep for hours. It felt like the most comfortable place in the world.

When I woke up, I watched him sleeping for a while. His beautiful lashes draped his face and his mouth was set in a soft smile as though he was dreaming of something pleasant. The man even slept in a good mood.

He woke up when they served the meal, and I asked him the question that had been bothering me since I'd met him. "How did you become an alcoholic?"

He stretched and looked out the window. Finally he looked back at me and said, "Oh, you don't want to hear about that."

"Yes, I do. I don't understand alcoholics. I've always thought of them as worthless drunks who can never live a normal life, but you and Josh have blown that idea to pieces. You both have more together than most people I know."

His eyebrows rose and a slight grin turned up the corners of his mouth, "I'm not sure how to take that. You see me as somewhere between a worthless drunk and someone who has it together. I don't think I'm either one."

"Well, what are you?"

"Just a normal sinner saved by grace, just like you."

"Yea, but I never had a big rebellion. I was always a good girl who obeyed the rules."

"Yes, but you knew the rules. I didn't. And even if I had, I don't know if I was motivated enough to keep them."

"What do you mean?"

"I never went to church until I was an adult, so I didn't know the rules. But just going to church wouldn't have done it for me. I needed an encounter with the living God."

"How did that happen?"

"It's a long story."

"This is a long flight."

"Okay," he sighed, taking a bite of his processed chicken and chewing it carefully. "My dad left the family when I was thirteen. I know that's not too unusual, but when my dad left, he really left. He went to Italy to do research on a book, and he never came back. We found out a few years later that he married some Italian woman, and that I have a half brother named Marcus.

"My mom had to go back to work, leaving me and my brother pretty much on our own. I started going to lots of parties on weekends because our home was a sad place. My mom never really got over my dad leaving like that, and she spent most of the weekend working overtime so she wouldn't have to come home to a house without him.

"So, at first the drinking was social, but then I started bringing extra bottles home from the parties and hiding them under my bed. I drank them warm to get to sleep at night. By the time I was in college, the only way I could cope with the pressure was with a drink. I only drank at night, so I as able to function during the day well enough to ace my classes. Most people didn't know I drank, only my roommate.

"My senior year, my roommate told a guy on our floor named Mike that he was worried about my drinking. Mike invited me to go to church with him and there I encountered God for the first time. After several months of going I gave my life to Christ, feeling that I'd waited my whole life for this."

"So then you gave up drinking?"

"Not yet. I knew I needed to, so I started attending an AA group at the church. It was those friends who helped me through the hard process of giving it up for good."

"Is it ever hard now? I mean are you ever tempted to drink again?"

"No, it's not tempting at all. I'd never go back to that state. I hated my dependence on alcohol. I think being an alcoholic made me understand being set free from my sins more than most people."

"What if you're around alcohol?"

"That can be tough, so I stay away. But it wasn't as though I was giving anything up as much as gaining a whole new life. I'd never want to trade that. The joy and pleasure I know in Christ beats any kind of buzz I could get from a drink."

"You know, for the first time, I think I understand how all our sins are equally bad to God. I never had any visible habits to kick, but I try to get my satisfaction from things other than Christ and that's just as bad."

We sat quietly after that and ate our meal. I stole glances at Grant and appreciated him all the more. "Thanks for telling me your story," I whispered, then fell back to sleep on his shoulder.

Back at work, I found out that Mrs. Murphy had done a bang-up job, and that Mr. Hopkins was able to hire a new landscape designer who would start in a couple of weeks.

Cherry Cobbler

"Life will be easier for all of us," he said with a sigh of relief.

The idea that life would be easier lasted until Mrs. Vanderweide came in. "While you were running around the world enjoying yourself, Cherry, I've been in crisis."

"How amazing," I thought to myself. "I can't imagine you in crisis." I wanted to defend myself. I wanted to tell her that I was working in Nigeria, not just on a pleasure cruise. I wanted to tell her to go spend some time there herself, but instead I said, "What's wrong?"

"Bart has left me."

"Who?"

"Mr. Finster, the man I met at your church."

"Oh. So you were dating regularly?"

"Yes, we had five dates. It was the longest relationship I've had in years. I thought this was it."

"So what happened?"

"Who can say?" she almost swooned. "He said something about my lack of interest in spiritual things."

"You?" I couldn't help it. I had to say it. My sarcasm was totally lost on her though.

"Yes! Can you imagine? I'm a deeply spiritual person. He just didn't give it a chance."

"Yes, well, does this mean you won't be coming to church anymore?"

"Oh no, I'll be back. I like it there. People don't seem to care if I have money or not. They seem to really care about me." It was the most humble statement I'd ever heard her make.

"That's great, Mrs. Vanderweide. I'm very glad." And I was.

It was hard to go back to worrying about people's yards after tending to someone who's dying of AIDS. I felt as if I'd been abducted by aliens to a planet that had great suffering then brought back to my privileged planet that didn't know what to do with itself other than spend money. It seemed to me as if all people were like the ones dying of AIDS at their core, but that here they dressed up in such fine clothes, houses, and cars that they didn't know their desperate state. And for that perspective, if nothing else, I was glad that I thought that Todd was The One for a while.

Grant came to find me about lunchtime. "Can you take a break?"

Cherry Cobbler

I nodded. "Yes, I'm hungry. My days, nights, and mealtimes are so messed up that I'm not sure when I'm supposed to do everything."

"Well, it's noon, which is the recognized lunchtime in the US of A, so come eat."

"Yes sir!" I saluted. He rolled his eyes and walked to the Japanese maple and sat down. I joined him.

"So, are you doing okay? No broken heart or anything?"

"No broken heart. I'm doing fine. I found out what I should have known all along, that I should take people as they are and not make them into something in my own image. I'll leave that to God from now on."

Grant laughed. He always thought I was funny, bless him.

Roslyn called that night to see if I needed to talk, but I really didn't. It was great to have friends who were there for you. "Hey, I owe you a slug," she said after we established that I wasn't in pain.

"What are you talking about?"

"You promised me that I could slug you the next time you said you were in love."

"Ah, but technically, this was the same love as the last time, so you won't be able to collect on that one."

"You always have loopholes."

"That's me! I'm one big loophole. So, do you and Josh have a date yet?"

"Yes! It's going to be a December wedding. You get to wear red velvet."

I groaned. I pictured myself looking like an apple.

"No, you're going to love the style. It's very slimming."

"Okay," I said unconvinced.

"We'll go try one on this weekend. How about it?"

"You're on."

We did go, and she was right. The dress was slimming. I never knew I could wear red and look so smashing. It was quite dramatic and made me feel good about myself. We went out for lunch afterwards. "So Roslyn, how did you cope with all the wealth here when you came back from Romania?"

"It was a struggle. I think I've come to terms with it by being determined not to fall into the materialistic trap that is waiting for me at every curb."

"How do you do that?"

Cherry Cobbler

"I keep in touch with those in Romania for one. I hear from them at least every couple of weeks by email, which keeps me grounded to the way life is there."

"That's good; what else?" I felt like taking notes.

"When I start telling myself that I need something, I remind myself that it's really a want, not a need."

"Makes sense. Anything else?"

"Probably most importantly, I give away a ton of money. I make sure it doesn't have a hold on me."

"I like that. I've started giving more to church already and of course, to Todd's mission."

"That's great, Cherry. I can see that the trip was worth it, even if you didn't end up with a husband."

"I think I got something even better."

"What's that?"

"Perspective."

"And that's even better than a husband? Where's the Cherry I know, and what did you do with her?"

"Very funny. Yes, it's better, because even if God gives me a husband now, I'll have a better perspective of what to expect in a marriage and in life in general."

"Pretty profound."

"That's me. Soon everyone will be coming to hear my great pearls of wisdom."

"I wouldn't be surprised."

37

On Saturday when I went to the soup kitchen, I didn't even recognize it. All the appliances were state of the art; I'd never seen so much stainless steel in one place. The walls were rough-plastered and painted a warm brown to look as if they'd come from old Italy, and the counters were decorative tile. A rack hung from the ceiling with all new copper pots. Even the towels and dishrags were new.

I found Sylvia to see if she was happy or annoyed. She was somewhere in between. "Cherry, how dare you run off to Africa and leave me with that exasperating man!" I felt a little like ducking, she spoke so strongly, but then she changed her tone to one of awe. "But have you ever seen a more beautiful kitchen in all your life?" And I knew it was okay.

"Not ever!" I exclaimed as enthusiastically as possible.

"The worst part wasn't even that weird little man, it was the press."

"Were they here a lot?"

"Only about twenty different publications. You would have thought we were Buckingham Palace. I've never answered so many questions. Every time I stepped out of the kitchen, a microphone was shoved in my face. If it had gone on any longer, I would have shoved a microphone or two down someone's throat."

"It is pretty amazing that they got it done so fast," I ventured, trying to calm her down.

"That was the one thing I insisted on with Rolf." She pointed her finger at me as if Rolf was my best friend, "Do you know I don't even think his name is Rolf. I bet it's Ralph, and he didn't think it sounded sophisticated enough, so he changed it. I started calling him that at the end and oh, did it make him mad!" She laughed heartily at the memory. "I said it really obnoxiously too. Boy was it fun to see him wince!"

"Well, I'm glad you were able to have a little bit of fun with the whole thing."

She was thoroughly enjoying herself now. "Oh, I did! You know what I did on his last day?"

I shook my head.

"I stuck a sign on his back that said 'Call me Ralph'." She was now so tickled that she could hardly finish the story. "I had everyone here saying it with great relish." Then she leaned toward me and whispered, "I thought it was nicer than a sign that said 'kick me', which is what I really wanted to do."

Cherry Cobbler

I smiled. "At least it's all over, and you have a brand new kitchen."

"Yep, it's mighty fine, as my grandmother would have said. Mighty fine." And she walked away with a pleased look on her face.

As I got to work, I was surprised that Gloria actually approached me and spoke. "So you went to Africa?"

I nodded.

"What was it like?"

"Mostly poor and hot, but parts of it were beautiful and the people were lovely."

She stood there, pondering what I'd said and I thought our conversation was done until she added, "I'd like to go to Africa sometime." Then the conversation did end because she moved to her station as we began to serve.

Later at the break, I resumed it. "So, why do you want to go to Africa?"

She shrugged her shoulders, obviously sorry that she'd mentioned it. "Why not?"

"Why there and not Switzerland or Jamaica?"

She blew a bunch of air out as she waved her hand in disgust. "Bunch of rich people there. Rather go to Africa."

And that seemed to explain it all.

Crystal came to see me that afternoon, roaring up in her convertible then banging on my door as if she were afraid I'd died. "So, why didn't you tell us you were going to Africa?" she cried as soon as she was inside.

"It happened rather suddenly."

"This about that guy?"

I nodded. She frowned, "So what happened?"

"It didn't work out."

She sat down as if intending to give me a long counseling session. "I could have told you that; saved you going half way around the world."

"I guess I should have asked," I said, just to keep her happy.

"Yes, you should have. I'm pretty good with these things."

It was time to change the subject. "So how's my niece slash nephew?"

She patted her stomach that was just starting to pooch. "Just fine. I haven't even been sick."

Cherry Cobbler

"I'd like to give you a baby shower," I blurted. Where did that come from? It was as if aliens took control of my mouth and I spoke against my will. That happens to me a lot. But her expression made me glad, for once.

"You would do that for me?" She jumped off the sofa and grabbed me in a hug. "You are the sweetest thing in the whole world. You are a true sister, the one I always wished I had."

What could I say to that?

I worked hard and managed to get a few of my friends there. I found out that Crystal actually had some friends too. And since my mom and Crystal's mom both attended, we had about a dozen people in my apartment, which had been transformed into a baby paradise. I knew Crystal wouldn't be happy unless it looked like an advertisement for Baby World, so I'd gone all out with floral arrangements that included baby booties and bibs, and balloons tied to everything that could hold some without floating to the ceiling.

Crystal's mom was named Queenie. Whether that is her real name or a nickname, I have never been able to discover, but it fit her the way a glove fits a hand.

If Crystal makes a dramatic entrance, her mother has a five-star band trumpeting her arrival. Queenie came dressed in an outfit that looked as if it had been designed with Cher in mind. It had more glitter, sequins and feathers than I thought any amount of fabric could hold. She burst into the room carrying a package that looked as if it contained a small pony, which really wouldn't have surprised me very much had that been the case.

She made a great display of hugging and kissing everyone in the room, even though she didn't know half of them. When she got to Roslyn, the poor little doctor looked at me as if she'd like to perform surgery on me in my sleep.

As Queenie made the rounds Crystal whispered to me, "Isn't my mother wonderful? I hope I'm just like her when I'm that age." I stared straight ahead, the mental picture too horrible to visualize.

When Queenie finally sat down, she sat at the edge of her seat, looking around the room as if she were indeed a monarch surveying her kingdom. As I held my breath, she gestured my way, "Lovely decorations, Cherry." And I sighed with relief that she didn't say, "Off with her head."

My mother, who was as practical as the day is long, sat next to her and chatted amiably. I figured that the thought of a grandchild had made everything right with the world, even Queenie.

I asked Roslyn if she would start the shower with a short devotional on the blessing of children and a prayer for Crystal's baby. I held my breath as she began to share, because I was pretty sure that neither Crystal nor

Cherry Cobbler

Queenie knew what a Bible was, although they might have heard of a person who prays.

She gave a lovely talk about how she'd come to love children through her time in Romania and then shared some verses that explained what a blessing from the Lord children were. I was afraid to look at my sister-in-law, so I kept my eyes glued on Roslyn. She finally closed praying that God would help Crystal's baby to be healthy and strong and that He would lead the little one to Himself.

I'd barely opened my eyes when Crystal and her mother jumped up at the same time and surrounded Roslyn in a big hug. "That was the most beautiful thing I've ever heard," Crystal exclaimed with tears in her eyes. "It certainly was," her mother echoed. "May I have that prayer in writing? I'm going to pray it every day for my grandchild."

I blinked in surprise. Who would have guessed?

38

Something changed in Crystal's and my relationship after the shower. The idea of a baby that would be a part of our family sunk in and made me feel differently about her. Her gratefulness about the shower warmed my heart, and even Queenie made herself believable as a grandmother. I felt hopeful.

At work a few days later, Crystal happened to stop by while Mrs. Vanderweide was there. They both stared at each other as if they were long lost sisters separated at birth. Striking up a conversation with each other, they found out they had more in common than the Dixie Chicks. Crystal was fascinated that Mrs. Vanderweide had her own makeup line, and Mrs. Vanderweide thought Crystal would make a wonderful model in her makeup commercials. It was a match made in heaven or the other place, I'm not sure which.

They both left together, and I had a small hope that perhaps they'd leave me alone now.

Since my mother had come for the shower, she decided to stay the week which would have been wonderful except that I had to work every day and she was starting to go stir-crazy sitting in my apartment.

So far she'd made thirteen varieties of cookies and froze them all so we wouldn't eat them in one sitting. She also painted my bathroom a rather obnoxious color of greenish-blue that I would have never chosen. It made me think that perhaps she should go to work for Rolf. But the final straw was that she threw away the tab curtains that I'd loved and saved for and replaced them with frilly gingham ones that she'd made.

When I came home and saw them, I couldn't help it. I cried. "I thought you'd be happy!" she cried in self-defense. "I wanted to surprise you."

"What did you do with my old ones?"

She looked rather sheepish. "I put them in the dumpster."

"You what?"

"They were really faded."

"That was how they came. It's a certain look that's popular now, Mother. I paid a fortune for those!"

With that knowledge, my mother's sympathy was gone. "Well, you got cheated."

"I'm going to get them back!"

I stormed out of the house, down to the dumpster, and flipped the lid open so forcefully that it slammed against the back and reverberated through the buildings. I found an old wooden box to stand on and leaned in. There at the bottom, sitting in some unidentifiable garbage goo, were my curtains. I leaned over to reach them, but couldn't, so I stormed into the house, grabbed a broom and went back out. With the broom, I fished them out, which was a good word to use because they smelled just as if I'd pulled them from a swamp. Evidently the goo was from a fermented fish or two.

I took them to the laundry room, threw them in and started the cycle. It said clearly on the label to dry clean them, but there was no way that a dry cleaner could get that smell out. Then I marched back into my apartment and found my mother calmly looking through a magazine.

"Mother, we have to get something straight around here." I was aware that I bore a resemblance to a snorting bull at the moment.

She didn't even look up, but patted the chair, saying in her best "mother" voice, "Sit down, Cherry, you're giving me a headache."

I knew that tone. I would have to sit and talk reasonably, or I'd get nowhere. It was a lesson I'd learned in kindergarten when I'd thrown a fit about a dress she'd given away that was too small for me. So I sat down and prayed for my voice to be the right tone so that she'd listen. It took enormous self-control. "Mother," I said as sweetly as possible.

It must have been acceptable, because she looked up. "Mother," I repeated, "I love you."

"I love you too, dear."

I ignored that. "And I love having you visit me. I love each and every cookie you made, and I can live with the bathroom, even though I feel like I'm in somebody's pool." She started to say something, but I put my hand up to stop her. "But throwing my curtains away is stepping over a line."

"But..."

"I'm not done yet, Mother. Let me finish." I kept my voice calm, even though I felt like standing on the table and using a megaphone. "Now, I realize that you spent a lot of time making the ones that are presently on my windows, and that you thought I'd like them. But you know what, I don't."

"Really," she said dryly.

"Those curtains are you, Mom. They aren't me. The other curtains are me. How would you like it if I came to your house and threw away all your curtains and put up mine?"

She'd been about to say something, but this gave her pause. I could see I'd struck a chord. She looked at me for a full minute, then said, "You're right, Cherry, and I was wrong. I'm sorry."

I'll say one thing for my mom. She's fair. "No more changing things without my permission?"

She nodded. "What should we do about these curtains?"

"Can you use them at home?"

"No, I have all the curtains I need."

"I tell you what. I'll take them with me when I go to the soup kitchen and see if anyone wants them."

My mom brightened up at that suggestion. "Good idea. By the way, your soup kitchen looks beautiful."

"When did you see it?"

"It was on our six o'clock news at home."

I should have guessed.

The curtains turned out all right. They needed to be ironed about four times in a row, but my mother did that while I was at work. When I came home the next night, they were all back in place and just a little more faded than before, which I kind of liked. My mother just shook her head when I told her so, but we'd agreed to disagree a long time ago about a great many things.

Cherry Cobbler

The one thing we didn't disagree on was food, and the best part about having Mom there was all the wonderful meals she had waiting for me when I got home. There was something about a meal together that always helped Mom and me to relax and talk. "So, Cherry, are you sure you don't want me to set you up with Edgar?"

"Perfectly sure, Mother," I answered firmly as I put a large piece of potato in my mouth. "I think I'm through with men," I added after I'd swallowed.

My mother just smirked and changed the subject. "Anything new at work?"

"Not right now, but we're getting a new designer in a week or two."

"Male?" she asked hopefully.

"Female," I answered decisively to put to rest any further inquiry in that direction.

"Oh." She seemed to lose interest in the conversation. "Your father and I are going to Europe," she said as casually as if she'd said "I'm going to the supermarket."

I stopped chewing. "You're kidding! What made you decide to do that?"

"Two things," and she held up two fingers in case I didn't know what the word *two* represented. "One, your trip to Africa got us thinking that we'd never really traveled.

We've wanted to go to Europe since before we were married."

"What's the other thing?"

"Sam and Crystal's baby."

"Sam and Crystal's baby makes you want to go to Europe?" I couldn't see the connection.

She nodded, "Yes, we both knew that as soon as we had a grandchild that there is no way we'd want to leave the country, so we have to go now."

"I think that's great, Mom. You guys deserve it."

"Oh, I don't know if any of us ever deserve anything, but I'm grateful we get to go."

"Will you send me a postcard?"

"One from every port."

"I love you, Mom."

"I love you too, Cherry blossom."

Mom wanted to entertain my friends so on Friday night Roslyn, Josh, Grant, Jacqueline, and Mrs. Murphy came over. I loved it that Mrs. Murphy and I were friends. Sometimes it helped to have an older woman who wasn't my mother around, and she was the wisest woman I knew.

Anyway, Mom went all out. She fixed a good old-fashioned meal of pot roast complete with potatoes, carrots, and onions. But best of all was the homemade bread and freshly baked apple pies. Everyone was hungry as soon as they walked in the door.

Nobody appreciated it more than Grant, who charmed my mother instantly by bringing her flowers. "Mrs. O, this is the best meal I've had in a year, maybe two years." My mother reveled in praise for her cooking. "Why you poor boy, don't you have anyone to cook for you?"

"Nope, I live alone, and all I know how to cook are microwave meals. I think I've tried them all, and I'm sick of every one."

"That's terrible!" My mother can't imagine a worse fate than living off of microwave meals. "I tell you what; I planned on fixing some meals and freezing them for Cherry. I'll just make double so you can have some too."

"Wow! That's the nicest thing any one's every offered to do for me. You're the greatest."

After that Grant could do no wrong as far as my mother was concerned. Everything he said was funny and intelligent, every gesture he made thoughtful. By the end of the evening, she'd adopted him as a son, promising to send baked goods regularly and offering their home as a getaway when he needed a break. I was surprised she didn't ask him to move in with them.

When the evening ended, my mother buttonholed me. "What in the world are you doing going all over the world looking for a man when you have that gorgeous person right at your doorstep?"

"Grant?" I asked like a dummy.

"Yes! Why haven't you told me about him? He's got everything. He's good-looking, charming, intelligent, sweet, and could really make a woman's blood boil," she said in a conspiratorial way as she nudged me with her elbow. I hated it when my mom talked like that. Daughters don't like to think that their mothers know anything about blood boiling.

"I know Grant's all those things, but he's just a friend. It would be like having a thing for my brother."

"Believe me Grant is nothing like your brother."

She certainly had a point there. "That's true." I decided to take another angle. "Don't worry, Mom. After tonight, Grant's probably in the family anyway. He's as taken with you as you are with him."

"I hope so. Your dad would like him too. Do you know that Grant likes to fish? Think of what fun they'd have."

Cherry Cobbler

"They would indeed. Let's get this mess cleaned up."
And we spent the rest of the evening washing dishes and reminiscing about simpler times.

I missed Mom a lot after she left. I even smiled when I bathed in my tropical looking bathroom, expecting to see a jellyfish swimming next to me. I was really tired of living alone.

39

Josh, Roslyn, Grant, and I all went to an AA meeting. Since I'd talked to Grant about his past, I'd grown curious. I asked Roslyn if she'd go too, and she jumped at the chance.

It was a pretty amazing experience. Grant and Josh began greeting people right away when they walked in. They asked several people how their week had gone, so I assumed those they talked to were in the new, fragile stage.

Roslyn settled in to watch, so I joined her towards the back of the room. We didn't say much, just took in our surroundings. Several people welcomed us and it dawned on me for the first time that they probably thought we were alcoholics. It was a weird feeling, but I didn't feel horrified at the idea. I figured that must mean I'd made some progress in my attitude.

As different people got up to talk, I began praying earnestly for them. I wanted them to make it the way Grant and Josh had. I wanted them to have a great life and not be stuck anymore. I could see the relief some of them felt by being a part of a group like this. Others looked terrified and about to bolt. I prayed the hardest for them.

When the meeting was over, the four of us went out to eat. "Thanks for taking us, guys. It was enlightening."

Roslyn nodded. "I kept seeing you up there, Josh. It's hard for me to believe you ever struggled like that. You seem as solid as Gibraltar now."

Josh laughed. "Wow, that's pretty solid." He picked up her hand and caressed it with his thumb. "I've come a long way. It's great to be on the other side. I'm just glad my brothers never fell into substance abuse. I guess they watched me and learned the easy way."

"You know, the past just doesn't weigh on a Christian the way it does on others," Grant added. "It's really true that our sins are buried in the deepest ocean."

"With a 'no fishing' sign posted." I'd heard that somewhere and liked it, so I thought I'd put my two cents' worth in.

"That's good, Cherry. I'll remember that. That would be a good thing to share with some of the people at AA, wouldn't it, Grant? It's a good visual picture."

"It sure is. Cherry's great at visual pictures. She'd make a terrific motivational speaker."

"No way," I almost yelled. "Traveling around telling people how to live their lives would be terrifying."

Grant chuckled. "I never thought about it that way. It would be quite the challenge."

"I know," Roslyn said, "we could all go to Romania and start an AA chapter. Alcohol's a big problem there."

"You seem to forget that Grant and I aren't going to live in Romania, my dear," I reminded her.

"Well, you could."

Grant caught my eye and grinned. "What do you say, Cherry? We're now experienced missionaries." Then he turned to Roslyn, "Do they like elephant jokes in Romania?"

I roared with laughter, and Josh and Roslyn looked at us as though we were ready for the men in the white coats.

When I'd finally pulled it together I asked Josh, "Speaking of Romania, what are your plans when you get there. Are you going to assist Roslyn in surgery, or what?"

"Actually, I'm going to get some more medical training while we're there. Medical school in Romania is not as tough to get into or nearly as expensive as it is here."

"So we'll be Mr. Doctor and Mrs. Doctor," Roslyn added. That was about as close as she got to a joke, so I tried to laugh in support of her.

"What about your brothers, Josh?" I couldn't help but ask.

Cherry Cobbler

"What about them?" He looked confused.

"How do they feel about you going so far away?"

"They're a little sad, but they've all promised to visit. My youngest brother is thinking about practicing with us for a while."

"Wow, that would be great."

Roslyn smiled, "It sure would. I love your brothers."

"Of course you do," he said. "They remind you of me."

"Uh oh, they're getting mushy, Cherry. What should we do about it?" Grant teased them, but he was obviously enjoying them.

"It's hopeless, Grant. They are too much in love." And on that happy note, we decided to call it a night.

The new landscape designer arrived perky and shiny on Monday morning. Just a few years out of college, she was five foot two, about a size two, and looked like she was twelve years old. What she lacked in size, she made up for in enthusiasm. This girl could sell water lilies in the desert.

On her very first day, she actually made an appointment to meet Mrs. Vanderweide. Within the hour, she'd managed to convince her that Mr. Hopkins' latest plan for her yard was perfect, without letting her try one single shade of lipstick on her. The girl was good!

The only thing I didn't like about her was that her name was Sherry. Sherry and Cherry working in the same building sounded like two new flavors of Hostess cupcakes. I considered asking her if she wanted to join me in a new ice cream line.

"So Sherry, what brought you to our little corner of the world?"

The little darling answered in dripping southern tones, "I just wanted to work at the best place I could find. Landscaping is my dream and I knew this place had a great reputation."

"Are you ready for our winters?"

"Sure I am, Cherry. I went to school up here. I'm a regular Northerner now."

Right, I thought, and I'm from Manchester, England. You'll have to live here a long time to lose that accent. But of course being the civilized person I am, I in no way said such a thing out loud. Instead I said, "Do you know anyone in town?"

Her face drooped a bit, the only sign I'd seen that she wasn't happy every minute of the day, "No, that part may take a while."

Cherry Cobbler

"Well, I'm really involved in my church. We have a cookout tonight. Do you want to come? Church is a great place to meet people."

Sherry smiled wide and chased away any evidence of the blues, "I'd love that! I am a Southerner at heart still, and my mama would be pleased to hear I went to church. She's afraid the north will make a heathen out of me."

"Okay, I'll pick you up at six o'clock. Will that give you enough time?"

"Can I bring store-bought food?"

"I've got it covered this time. You can come as my guest."

"That's lovely, Cherry. You're sweet as molasses."

Personally, I don't like the taste of molasses but I knew she meant well.

Sherry came out looking like she was going to be doing a fashion shoot for *Vogue*. She had on a short jacket that fit her like a glove, accenting that teeny figure. She'd managed to put her hair up in a cute little do that looked like a salon had worked on it all afternoon. Even her makeup was fresh. I gave a sigh and welcomed her grandly.

She was a hit immediately. Both males and females flocked around her like so many birds around a feeder.

New people always got attention at church, but this seemed a bit overboard to me. Then again, I remembered how I'd acted around Todd and told myself to shush.

By the time we headed home I think she had at least three dates, but that didn't seem to satisfy her. "Who was that dark, smoky lookin' guy that kept talking to you?"

"That's Grant."

"He your beau?" The Deep South was coming out in full now.

I laughed, "Grant? No. He and I are just friends."

"So he's fair game?"

"All those men and you want Grant?" I felt a bit of panic for some reason.

"Yea, he's gorgeous!" She twirled her hair between two fingers, "He didn't seem to notice me, though."

"Grant's a funny bird… but a nice guy," I added quickly. "He's not like all the other men."

Sherry sank lower in her seat and giggled, "I think so too." Then she straightened up, "Will you help?"

"How?"

Cherry Cobbler

"I don't know. Feel him out for me. Throw some hints. Heck, just ask him outright if you want."

"I don't think I can do that," I said looking for some reason why not.

"How come?"

"I'm not a good matchmaker. I'd rather stay out of that business," I fudged. "He works at the garden center, you know." I had to add that, or she'd wonder why I didn't.

"No kidding! Wow, I'll just flirt with him tomorrow, then." We pulled up to her apartment building, and she bounced out with as much energy as she'd started work with that morning. I watched her go and felt like crying.

I called Roslyn as soon as I got home. "Can you come over?"

"Sure, what's wrong? You sound as though you've lost your best friend."

"I think I might have."

"What? I thought I was your best friend."

"Just come over."

Her kidding died on the phone as she answered soberly, "Okay."

She knocked on my door fifteen minutes later. A true friend. I pulled her in and sat down on the sofa still holding her hands. "I'm in love with Grant."

"What?"

"I am; it's true. I didn't know it until today, but I'm in love with him."

"For heaven's sake, Cherry, you thought you were in love with Todd a few months ago." Her voice was anything but gentle, even though I was obviously close to tears!

"I know, but I wasn't."

"And why is this any different?"

"Because I thought Todd was someone he wasn't. I realize now that I wanted him to be like Grant."

"And what brought about this great revelation?" She was talking loud enough for the neighbors to hear.

"Sherry," I said as softly as she was loud.

If Roslyn had been a swearing woman, I'm sure she would have let off some steam that way now. "And who in Sam Hill is Sherry?"

"She's the darling new landscape designer at work."

"And?"

Cherry Cobbler

"And she is attracted to Grant."

"Well of course she's attracted to Grant. He's a gorgeous guy. Half the female population is attracted to Grant!"

"Really?" I was truly astonished.

"Yes, really." Roslyn was as mad as I'd ever seen her. She'd been through dozens of romances with me, but I'd never seen her so exasperated. "If you hadn't been so wrapped up in Todd, you would have noticed before now."

"Well, now I've noticed, and it's too late," I wailed.

That seemed to do it. Roslyn finally calmed down. She sighed as if the weight of the world was on her shoulders. "Cherry, why, besides Sherry, do you think you're in love with Grant?"

That was a topic I suddenly loved. The reasons flowed from my lips. "He's sweet, charming, thoughtful, polite, caring, and he has a great sense of humor. He understands me, and I understand him. He's as comfortable as an old shoe, but as fresh as a new spring day." I'd said all that calmly, but now I wailed again. "And he's going to fall for that little Barbie doll at work."

Roslyn took my shoulders firmly in hand, "You don't know that. Until you do, I'd suggest you look for an opportunity to talk to Grant about it. Since you're such great friends, it shouldn't be so hard."

"Yes, it is! I wouldn't be able to stand it if he told me we were just friends. If he marries someone else, I'll have to move to Africa because I won't be able to handle it." I was getting really close to being hysterical.

Roslyn refused to listen. "Fine, move to Africa."

I looked up in surprise, wondering what was up. She just stared at me with her eyebrows almost to her hairline. "What?"

"It's either talk to him or move to Africa. You choose." Then she got up and left. I spent the rest of the night staring at the ceiling.

40

The next day at work, I was so tired I could hardly keep my eyes open. But I woke up fast when I saw Sherry outside talking to Grant. I jumped up and went to the window, wishing I could hear what was going on. She was saying something that he evidently found hilarious, because he was laughing uproariously. A few minutes later she handed him a piece of paper that I was terribly afraid had her phone number on it. He put it in his pocket and watched her walk away. There was a contented smile on his face. I walked back to my desk and put my head down. I would have fallen asleep if I weren't crying so much.

Around lunchtime, I decided to find Grant and see if he'd have lunch with me, but I couldn't find him anywhere. I finally asked Lucy in retail. "Oh, he went out with that new landscape designer. She was clinging to his arm like English ivy. They would make a cute couple," she said cheerfully. I wanted to wring Lucy's neck.

At the end of the day I looked for him again, but he was nowhere to be found. Sherry, however, seemed to be everywhere. "Cherry, I didn't even need your help. I met Grant all on my own and we had lunch together. He's an absolutely delightful guy. I can't imagine that no one has snatched him up yet. I'm going for him."

I somehow managed a rather sick-looking smile. She noticed. "You look awful, Cherry. Are you coming down with something? You'd better go home to bed."

I nodded and thought that was exceptional advice. I went home and actually went to bed without supper. I had to be in love because I'd never done that before.

I finally had the chance to talk to Grant a couple of days later. I tried to keep my voice light. "So, I've missed you at lunch lately. You never seem to be around."

He looked at me in surprise. "Yea, I've been gone around lunchtime," he said lightly. "You want to go with Roslyn and Josh to the movies this weekend? You can invite Sherry if you want. She seems lonely; doesn't really know anyone in town."

I wanted to hit him. How could I love someone so much and still want to hit him? But I did. I couldn't get any words out, so I just nodded then I changed my mind and shook my head. "Why don't you just ask her? I think I need to rest this weekend."

"Are you okay, Cherry? You don't look well." His voice was so tender it made me want to cry.

"No, I'm fine. Just tired. See you later, Grant."

Cherry Cobbler

"Bye, Cherry.

And there was something so final about the way he said it that I rushed to the bathroom and bawled.

I found out on Monday that Grant did ask Sherry to go with him. Sherry described it in glowing terms. "We ended up going to a play instead of the movies. I knew about one that was just opening downtown. He came in this incredible suit that looked as though it had been made for him. It made me want to kiss him then and there, but being a southern lady, I refrained." She gave a wicked smile that indicated that was a one-time consideration. "Your friend Roslyn is great, too. She and I got along like a house-a-fire." Oh great, I thought, she's stealing my best friend, too.

I smiled more vigorously this time. I'd been practicing.

"Well, I've got to get back to work, Cherry. It's been great talking to you."

Yea, about as much fun as sticking my head in an oven, I thought.

Roslyn called about an hour later. "Hi, Cherry. I'm on break. How are you doing?"

"Terrible, what do you think?" I wasn't even trying to be nice.

"Have you talked to Grant yet?"

"How can I? He's in the presence of Miss Wonderful every time I get near him."

"For heaven's sake, Cherry, just tell him you want to talk to him. You're good enough friends to do that."

"I can't. I'd just die if he told me he likes Sherry. It's pretty obvious he does, but I can't stand hearing him say it."

"So you're just going to keep on being miserable?"

"I don't have much choice, do I?" The other line rang. "I've got to go Roslyn."

"Okay. I'll call you later."

Grant stopped in a few hours later. "Cherry, I've missed you. Do you want to share some lunch? I have leftover stir fry to share from the weekend."

"You're not going out with Sherry?"

"What?" He looked confused.

"Out to lunch with Sherry?"

"No." He looked more confused than ever. I decided that he'd rather not talk about it with me. Who could blame him?

Cherry Cobbler

"Sure, I'll have some stir fry."

"Great! It's really good stuff. I got it at that new Chinese restaurant in town. We'll have to go there sometime. I think you'll like it."

I just nodded. "Are you all right, Cherry? You just don't seem yourself these days."

I nodded again, and he looked at me suspiciously. I couldn't speak because if I did, I'd grab him and say, "I love you, can't you see? I love you, and I can't stand it that you love Sherry!"

We had a pleasant lunch talking about everything and nothing, just the way we used to, but there was a huge barrier between us that I couldn't get around. I didn't see how I could keep working here. As soon as I got home, I began searching the want ads.

After looking through all of them, I couldn't stand it anymore. I decided that finding out the worst was better than continuing in this manner. I called Grant to see if we could go out for dinner after work and talk.

"What about?" It was a fair question.

"I'd rather not say. Is it okay to wait to bring it up when we're out?"

"Sure, Cherry. Is everything all right?"

"I don't know. That's why I need to talk to you."

"Now you've got me worried."

"I'm sorry, Grant. Don't worry. We'll talk tomorrow."

"Oh, by the way, your mom sent me some cookies. They are out of this world. Do you want me to bring some to work tomorrow?"

"No, you keep them. I've got all her recipes."

"Wow, that's a gold mine."

"You're sweet, Grant."

"Are you sure you're okay, Cherry?"

I had to get off the phone. "Yep. See you tomorrow," I said as cheerfully as I could muster. It's good that I'm used to drama.

The next day went slower than a turtle on a newly waxed floor. Fortunately, Sherry had a busy day so I was spared her gushing about how wonderful Grant is. In my state of mind, I might have done some kind of permanent damage.

Cherry Cobbler

At long last, the day's tasks ended and Grant showed up right on time in my office. "So, do you want to go home and change or just go as we are? I'm pretty grubby."

"You're wonderful. Let's go now."

"Great. Where do you want to go?"

"How about that little Italian place? It's quiet, and we won't be interrupted."

"Okay," he said with a voice full of doubt then added, "You're making me nervous. Did I do something wrong?"

"No! I'm sorry if I'm making you feel bad. I just need to talk to you." Poor guy. He had no idea what I was about to do. I felt like chickening out and running home.

We drove to the restaurant in silence, ordered quietly, and talked about nonsense. Grant tried to keep the conversation going. He wasn't used to me being silent and didn't know what to do about it. I obviously had him worried. "So what's up, Cherry?"

I took a deep breath and decided to plunge ahead. "What's going on with you and Sherry?"

"Who?"

"Sherry, our little southern belle at work."

"Oh, her. What do you mean?"

Why was he being so dense? "I mean, are you two serious about each other?"

"Sherry and me?"

I wanted to slap him, but I controlled myself and simply said, "Yes."

"No. What would give you that idea?

"Well, all the time you two spend together. The way you look at each other. The great time you had together last weekend."

Grant looked as if I'd accused him of an assassination plot. "You thought that I was interested in Sherry?"

"Why wouldn't you be? She's charming and pretty and she's crazy about you."

"She is?"

Oh great. He hadn't realized it and now I'd told him so that he could pursue her. What had I done? I nodded calmly, but I wanted to throw up.

"I had no idea." He shook his head and then looked up at me. "I see. You wanted to tell me so I wouldn't lead her on. I was just trying to be nice because she seemed lonely. I'll make sure first thing tomorrow that she understands there's nothing between us." He was becoming downright cheerful. "Thanks, Cherry, I really appreciate you looking out for me that way. You're the best friend ever."

He smiled a huge, warm smile and I fought tears.

I was one confused woman. I felt great relief that Grant didn't love Sherry, but almost as much despair that we'd continue to be just friends. Somehow I got through the rest of that dinner and managed to hide my emotions enough that Grant thought we were just fine.

At work the next day, I saw Grant talking to Sherry. She looked crestfallen and slowly walked away after a few minutes. He had a pained expression on his face. At least I'd saved her from more heartbreak, what little comfort there was in that.

Sherry came in to see me later in the day. If she'd had a good cry, she was over it now. "Well, guess what?"

"What?"

"Your friend isn't interested in me."

"I'm sorry, Sherry."

"You knew?"

"He told me last night."

"Why didn't you tell me?"

"I thought that he should."

"Yea, oh well. It's just my luck. I attract them like flies but have trouble holding them." She looked at me a minute. "I'll bet it's just the opposite with you. When a guy falls for you, he's probably loyal for life."

"I wouldn't know," I said quietly, hoping she wouldn't say anymore.

"This whole romance business is a puzzler. When you get it figured out, will you tell me?"

"It's a deal." All of a sudden I liked her again.

After work, Grant stopped in the office. "Well, I told her."

"Yea, we talked."

"Is she taking it okay?"

"Really well."

His face showed great relief. "Good. I'm not used to being in the heartbreaking business. I don't like it. I think I might go back to my old clothes and glasses."

I smiled and blurted before I could think, "I'd love you just as much if you did."

He looked as if someone had used him to test the theory of electricity. "Do you mean that?"

Cherry Cobbler

I smiled and nodded, but he kept staring at me as if I'd just said that I was from the planet Venus. He'd been standing, but now he pulled up a chair and sat. "Can we talk?"

"Sure." I had no idea what was coming.

"Can we talk about us?"

"Yes," I said, afraid to breathe again for fear this moment would go away.

He scooted closer to my chair until our knees were touching. "Cherry, I..." but whatever he was going to say got lost in a wave of emotion. He grabbed my hands and tried again. "Cherry, I don't think I can continue as merely your friend."

Whatever I'd expected, it hadn't been that. I frowned. "What do you mean?"

He looked away for a minute but continued to hold my hands. "I'm doing this badly." And then he turned toward me again gazing into my eyes as if he were about to get lost in them forever. There was no mistaking that look. "Cherry, I feel a lot more than friendship for you. I've tried to pretend that being your friend is enough, but it's just not. I want so much more."

My heart started beating so fast that I was slightly afraid I'd pass out. Once I got my breath back, all I managed to get out was "Oh."

His face looked as if I'd told him to jump off a bridge. "I'm sorry. I shouldn't be telling you this. It's not fair to you. I know you're just getting over Todd and..."

I didn't let him finish. I almost yelled, "No, I'm not!"

He looked shocked, "What?"

"I'm way over Todd."

"You are?

I nodded again, wishing I'd been an English major so that I could find some beautiful words to express what I wanted to say. "Ever since Sherry came, I've realized that it's you I've loved all along. I couldn't stand the thought that you might be with her, and that I'd lose you forever."

"Really?" To my surprise, he turned away for a moment and walked around the room, looking as though he was lost and couldn't find his way out. Then he walked back, took my hands again, and pulled me to my feet. Looking in my eyes and speaking with a voice that sounded as though someone were strangling him he said, "You love me?"

I couldn't believe the moment. I threw my arms around his neck and whispered in his ear, "I love you so much that I can't stand it."

He pulled me back to look in my eyes again, "I can't believe this is happening. I've loved you from the moment I met you and had almost given up hope."

Cherry Cobbler

I couldn't bear to look in his eyes again; they were so beautiful and the intensity of his expression took my breath away so I looked down. He carefully lifted my chin and wrapped me in a kiss that will last a lifetime.

HAPPILY EVER AFTERWARD

Crystal and Sam had a girl and named her Victoria. There was no doubt that she was destined for greatness, either as a monarch of a small country or a supermodel for a jungle line. Crystal turned out to be a devoted mother and amazingly sensible too. Even my mother was surprised.

Mrs. Murphy's daughter got married to a nice man who was planning to be a minister. You could not have found a prouder mother this side of Tokyo. The flowers at the wedding were unbelievable.

I got a letter from Todd about a year after I'd visited. He found a lovely bride who was already a missionary there. They got along great and were as happy as clams. Evidently she didn't know any elephant jokes.

Josh and Roslyn are now in Romania. They are becoming a famous duo there. You will probably hear about them in the news one of these days. We're going to visit next summer.

Mrs. Vanderweide never did find a man, but she keeps trying. She faithfully attends church and invites more people to Faith Church than she does to her parties. Mr. Finster is now married to a nice, conservative widow.

Sylvia still loves her kitchen. She's been able to raise tons of money for her cause because of all the publicity. We have the best network for homeless people on the face of the earth.

Gloria has only landed in prison a few more times. She's even accepted a ride home with me lately.

Jeannie was the most surprised of anyone at Grant's and my wedding announcement, but my mother was the happiest.

ABOUT THE AUTHOR

JoHannah Reardon blogs at www.johannahreardon.com. If you enjoyed this book, please give it a positive review. Also, check out her other books:

Christian Fiction: *Crispens Point, Redbud Corner, Gathering Bittersweet, Journey to Omwana, Prince Crossing*
Children's Fiction: *The Crumbling Brick*
Family Devotional: *Proverbs for Kids*

Read an excerpt from the historical novel *Gathering Bittersweet:*

"Rachel, Raacheel…" Fay's call jolted me out of my daydreams as I walked along the shore throwing pebbles into the rushing water. The peace I had been enjoying now shattered at the sound of her panic stricken voice. It had to be Papa. I picked up my skirts, wadding them in a knot by my hip so that I could run faster.

As I approached the house, breathless and frightened, I noticed an unfamiliar horse tied to our fence post. Entering, my eyes first rested on a quiet figure standing in the shadows at the corner of the room. Before my mind could dwell on the question of who it could be, my sister Fay embraced me as she sobbed uncontrollably. I turned my head slowly to look at our father, afraid to see the inevitable.

He laid so quietly, just a wisp of the big man who used to carry me on his shoulders when I was a child. I pulled myself from Fay's grip and walked hesitantly over to his bed. "Oh Papa!" was all I could manage to croak out of my raw throat.

I touched his hand and kissed his forehead, anxious to do these things before he turned cold.

Fay continued to cry, her hands covering her face as she stood helplessly in the center of the room. The figure in the shadows now moved over to Fay. He removed his hat as he nervously turned it around in his large work-worn hands.

"I'm sorry, Ma'am. I wish there was somethin' I could've done. Do you want me to fetch the parson?"

Fay pulled herself together through sheer force of will as I had seen her do countless times before. "Yes. Pastor Watson knew that we'd be needing him soon. Thank you ever so much for stopping."

With that, the strange man dropped his hat onto his head and rushed out of the house with a relieved look on his face.

Fay and I were alone, feeling like two baby birds whose mother was just shot out of the air. I knew Fay's tears were not for grief alone but fear for our future. We seemed to have nothing to say to one another at this awful moment.

Cherry Cobbler

Fay sank into a chair, leaning her head on her crossed arms. I went back outside to my beloved river but the rapid movement of the water, which had comforted me a moment before, now sounded harsh and demanding as if it were washing my life away with the current. My tears joined the flow of water surrounding me, making me feel as I did when it rained for days on end, listless, without a desire for anything. At the dawn of each day for seventeen years, I'd risen to my father's voice. Now I'd never hear it again.

I pulled my knees up to my chest, wrapping my arms around them and rocked myself back and forth, as a mother rocks a child. My body ached for someone larger and stronger to hold me and comfort me but there was no one, so my own two arms were all I could use to ease my pain. I don't know how long I remained in this position, except when I unwound myself I was so stiff that I could hardly move. When I finally stood, I thought of Fay. Guilt pushed me back to the house, although I felt that I never wanted to enter it again. All I really wanted to do was to put our small boat on the water and let the river take me where it would, but that would never do. I'd have to come back some day, so I might as well face it now.

When I stepped into the darkness of our kitchen, I was shocked to see Fay busy preparing dinner. "We might as well eat early. I've got to go into town and wire Emily. We are going to join her and Adam in Montana. I've given the entire matter a lot of thought. We can't stay here alone,

Rachel." Fay had that determined look, which defied any disagreement.

I nodded my head and began setting the table, amazed that she could cook dinner with our father growing cold in the next room. And I knew better than to argue with her. Even if I objected to joining our sister and her husband, it would matter little. Twelve years my senior, Fay raised me since our mother died when I was a baby. She made the decisions, even when Papa was alive.

"Who was that man, Fay?"

"Just a passer-by. Father saw him out the window and told me to call him in. By the time I returned he'd quit breathing." Fay's voice trailed off into a whisper as she fought her emotions. The quiver in her composure caused my throat to constrict and made further conversation impossible.

Somehow we got through that awful dinner. Without speaking, Fay shoveled the food into her mouth while I mostly stirred mine around the plate. Each time I got close to my mouth with a bite, my stomach flipped like a fish out of water. Fortunately Fay was too caught up in her own emotions to notice. I moved things around enough that it looked like I'd eaten a bit.

The parson arrived as soon as we finished dinner. His face looked as sober as if it had been his own father who had passed on. He stared at the ground most of the time and shook his head side to side repeatedly. Quoting Scripture

Cherry Cobbler

and murmuring condolences, his voice became a hum in my ears like a mosquito's buzz. Relief flooded over me as he and Fay solemnly made their way into the other room to make the funeral arrangements while I washed the dishes. As the water swished in the dishpan, my tears began again in earnest, turning the dishtowel into a giant handkerchief.

The day of the funeral was even worse. Folks from all over came to help us commit Papa to the dust. Some of them I hadn't seen in years, but the whole countryside turns out for a funeral. I hated repeating the same meaningless nonsense over and over to each person as they tried to "comfort me in my sorrow." None of them were very good at it, so I began to feel that I was in a dream state I couldn't shake. My emotions went numb that day. I quit crying and nodded to each person as they continued to mutter sayings they'd heard others impart during funerals of their own. You'd think with all that practice, someone would figure out something useful to say like "This is horrible, isn't it? I hate it" or "I can't think of anything to say at a time like this because there just isn't anything to say." Not that these words would really do anything except make me feel like people were being honest. The only good thing about the funeral is that by the end of it, the numbness had passed and I was so mad I could have kicked a mule. Mad felt better than sad, so I stayed there a while.

Not that anyone noticed. Fay continued on with our plans without consulting my feelings whatsoever. She noticed my banging things around a little more than usual, I know, because she said, "Stop that right now, Rachel. You're giving me a headache." So that was that. I had to be mad by myself.

She decided we'd go see our mother's brother, Uncle Charles, before settling in Montana. He lived in Illinois, two days of train travel from our home in Bevel, Missouri. We'd only been to see him once before in our lives, and I'd been pretty young then. I could recall him being a dignified, quiet man. The trip didn't sound very exciting. But then again, nothing sounded very exciting. I just couldn't find enthusiasm for anything. If I could, I would have given Fay a piece of my mind about what I wanted to do, but I had no idea what I wanted to do, so I let her lead me like a little lost lamb.

The day we left for the train station with all our worldly possessions in our trunks, I looked back at the only house I'd known. The new tenants arrived just as we were leaving. As they waved cheerfully at our passing buggy, my anger flared again. How dare they be so happy about our shattered lives! I knew that wasn't fair, but I chose to feel that way anyway.

I'll say this for the parson. He practiced what he preached. His buggy was the one taking us to the station. He unloaded our trunks himself and hugged us both as though we were long lost daughters, even though we barely knew him. He'd just recently moved to the area, and we were not regular churchgoers. I've got to admit that I felt warmly toward him at the moment.

We boarded the train without a backward glance as the steam rushed from the engine so loud I could barely hear the people talking next to me. As we pulled out of the station I watched the town, which I knew better than my own face, recede in the distance. As the sound of the train bumping over the rails filled my mind, I tried to shake off the numbness of the last few weeks. I hadn't yet learned that sorrow can make us wise if we let it do its work, therefore I found myself in a prison of my own making, seeing only that life as I had known it, was gone forever.

My mind wandered back to my father. In all my seventeen years, it was he who brought the joy into our daily tasks. Fay kept the order and the discipline, and Papa gave us laughter. I loved to sit by his side after a hard day of work and listen to his stories. My favorite was his account of when, as a little boy, he saw Abraham Lincoln pass in a carriage while he was visiting St. Louis. It brought a smile to my face now and broke my dismal mood as I thought of my father as a child, enchanted at seeing the president.

As I gazed out the window watching the fields pass in a blur, I tossed around questions like a flock of birds circling a field. Would I ever see him again? I wanted to think that Papa had gone to a better place but I had no basis for this assurance. I wanted to believe in God, yet mine was a vague belief. Inside I balled my fist and muttered, "Why,

God, did you take him?" When someone dies, whom can we blame but God? Yet even as I blamed him, I felt that I was shaking my fist in ignorance.

"Why do you do this to yourself?" I muttered under my breath. I'm not a moody personality so it always disgusts me when my disposition is overtaken by emotion, which had been pretty much a constant state for the last few weeks. I forced myself to think of something else. Maybe it would do me good to move about. I slipped out of my seat and walked up the aisle. It always made me feel like giggling when I tried to walk in a moving train. I was sure this must be how a toddler feels when he is taking his first steps.

I almost made it the length of the train when the railcar I was in careened sharply to the left. The motion threw me on top of a young man seated near me. I began to gather myself to rise; I knew by the burning on my cheeks that they had turned scarlet. I was sure of it when I looked this man in the face. His initial reaction had been one of surprise, but his expression changed as his smile spread across his face like a sunrise peeking over the horizon.

"Well, an angel from heaven has plopped upon my lap," he laughed. He was a handsome man with very blond hair; it had not browned as so many blondes do. His eyes were a cool, clear blue, and he had a fine chiseled nose. I could tell by his suit that he was a man of means, young though he be. He wore an air of complete confidence, as though he controlled all circumstances.

Cherry Cobbler

"I'm sorry—the train—I didn't mean to!" I stammered in humiliation. I now became aware of the other passengers looking at me in disapproval, although I detected a glimmer of amusement on an elderly man's face.

"Now, I don't think it's a bit awful. It made a dull ride a lot more interesting." I was at once both attracted to and repulsed by this gentleman, if gentleman indeed he was. I had an overriding feeling that I should get back to Fay as quickly as possible. This was not the kind of man with which one felt safe.

"I'm glad to have amused you for a moment, but I must get back to my sister," I responded acidly, more to assuage my wounded pride than out of contempt for this man.

"Now wait a minute," he reached for my hand as he spoke. "I don't even know your name."

"Rachel, Rachel Scott. I must go now," I answered more civilly this time, although I pulled my hand back as if a snake had bit it.

Trying to hurry down that rocking railcar was almost impossible, fearing each moment that I'd land on someone else's lap. What worried me more was that I felt his eyes following me all the way, sending quivers of fear up and down my spine. Whether this was a good or bad feeling, I wasn't sure.

When I reached Fay again, the humor of the situation struck me. I giggled to myself as I thought of the foolish picture I made and the look of shock on the young man's face. I decided not to tell Fay about the episode. It would only upset her. Later she would think it was funny, but now she would be concerned for my dignity and the propriety of it all. Yes, it would be a secret between that young man and me. I tucked my hair back into its tidy bun and smoothed my wrinkled skirts. I was already a mess. What a sight I would be after a day and a night on a train. That thought made me giggle again. Fay had been resting, but now she opened one eye to peer at me. I quickly sobered up on the outside but continued to chuckle within. Perhaps my trek through the railcars had helped my gloomy mood after all.

My thoughts began to slowly trickle in another direction, as the beginning of a waterfall wears a new path in the stone. Maybe change isn't so bad after all. Who knows what could be in store for me now? If Papa were alive, I would most certainly have spent my entire life in Missouri. Even if the circumstances for leaving were depressing, I was offered a new chance at life. In the astounding resilience of the young, the adventure of the unknown began to replace the loss of the familiar. To my amazement, it was not just relief but anticipation that gripped me when the conductor announced our stop in Wesley, Illinois.

CPSIA information can be obtained at www.ICGtesting.com
Printed in the USA
LVOW092359100712

289587LV00006B/16/P